The Chameleon's

Last Dance

(a short escapade about the joys of dancing –

a bag of glees and good tidings)

KEITH BRAZIL

DEDICATION

To the Experimentals

To the Goddess Una

To all the dancing bears, queens and those lost in music

To the Skateboarding Kids surfing for runaway freedom

To the Rightness of Things

KEITH BRAZIL

CONTENTS

ACKNOWLEDGMENTS

Editor: Kitty Malone

Cover Design: Adam Wiltshire

Rose Illustration: Colin Francolino-Scott

With special thanks to my creative team for all their support and hard work: Kitty, Adam, Jason, Colin F-S, Stephen and to all those who have inspired me along the dancing way especially – Michael, Teresa, Jane & Michael, Simon, Nickie, Hannah, Susanna, Isabel, AMP & all my former dance buddies, my Dance & English teachers, Neil, Mark, Jim, Chris R, Tom, Mike M, Adrian, Rolf, Colin R, Tall Steve, Rami, Paul H, Bruce, Phil, Tony, Sean, Adam, Paul, Hendrik, Paul E, Gary, Billy, Rick, John, James, James McK, Adnan, Torsten, Igor, Brendan, Nick, Bob, Ed, Martin, Mark H, Carlos, Leandro, John, Angus, Paul, Ant, Mike B, Andy, Dave, Graham, John, Richie, Ben, Alf, Julian, Robert F, Alberto, Klaus, Stefan, Rudi, Gary, Mike D, Sean D, Eric, Francis, Karl, Andrea, Roger, Craig, Greg, Gary, Charles, Ben G, Nick W, Adan, Stephen, Seb, Trev, Andy, Hamish, Mario, John, Brian, Leather Mike, Ray, Wellington, Denny, & to all those who danced the nights away at the RVT & XXL.

A Rose Pink Production

The Chameleon's

Last Dance

(a short escapade about the joys of dancing –

a bag of glees and good tidings)

"He called a little child to him, and placed the child among them. And he said: "Truly I tell you, unless you change and become like little children, you will never enter the kingdom of heaven. Therefore, whoever takes the lowly position of this child is the greatest in the kingdom of heaven."

Jesus – Matthew 18:2-4
New International Version (NIV)

"…Change

and become like little children,

then will you enter the Kingdom of Heaven…"

(rewritten – K B)

Mok'sha – n.: *The liberation or the release (mukti) of soul*

(atma) from the bondage of the body

Namaste.

In the late December disco debris, under a projected Harvest Moon, I shuffle past the outer edges of the dance floor queuing on the way in to Club Land. As I wait, I watch some passing partygoers go by and look for early damage and delight. There are those dealing with the shards of Shattered Realities like a Christmas bauble that has been dropped or crushed beyond repair. ....*Soon turned out to be a heart of glass*... It might have been a relationship collision causing collateral damage, a pile-up of outworn wants and fervent wishes, or perhaps an accidental clashing of connectivity and craziness. Would-be bunny boilers abound. It could even be an incident as simple and brutal as the cutting of a thread like an unwanted passing. For their loss it is presently the worst time of year, as the cheeriness of others disturbs and they continue to struggle with the Moon's illusions and the Star's hopes for Life.

Some revellers, however, are testing a new found Love whilst others experience the Cup's sudden tipping in the tasting of too much Happiness that can turn to debauchery or disappointment. ...*People hold on...hold on*... It can be one or more of the Ten Thousand of Happy-Sad Things that disturb our sojourn on Earth. A few, even, house thoughts of leaving life early as, unbeknownst to them, they send

S.O.S. and distress signals out like auric flares, which explode like pulled party poppers streaming into the holographic air.

...Oh no, never give up, never give up, never give up...

Others are just highly-wired, seemingly plugged into the Christmas party circuit on some kind of dangerous, excitable overload. Like lights in a series, I know that if one goes we all blow, so I make sure I earth my electrics before take-off. Some Screaming Lads and Lassies on late liquid lunch pass us by in search of extra sugars and caffeine to keep them buzzing, eyeballs popping and dancing on stalks from the night before. Their jaws work overtime.

Still waiting impatiently in the ticket queue I am already on my eager toes, leaning on the shoulders of those in front. Balancing like a Meer Cat, listening and watching, I up periscope on the lookout, searching with an Observing Eye that flickers like a lighthouse. In between the flashes of breaking light and engulfing dark, I keep one ear to the ground and the other to the sky for earthly clues and cosmic gossip; information is swiftly gathered from both garrulous and silent tongues alike. My Coastal Guard and my Beloved's Paramedic are on early stand-by, going where the need takes us, but sometimes it is hard to say what it is that we find in amongst our own dancing fun.

Easy listening sounds from the back bar float by as doors swing open and close. Some passing punters disrobe, pulling off their shirts and tucking them under belts and into the tops of jeans. One attempts to tie his shirt around his waist, but it falls onto the floor. Messy already, he does not notice so we pick it up and hand it back to him, folded and ready to go. Later on, responsibility for rescuing lost T-shirts will turn temporarily to the saving of people. Caring is an attractive quality and becomes the man who can; gay fathers and friends often step up to the mark if they are not already up to their necks in wiping kids' arses, blowing noses or resolving teenage tearaway dramas.

Shuffling forward in the queue I pay the man sitting in the entrance Kissing Booth my money and he lets me in with a little cheeky peck and a solid Irish laugh. He is always up for the 'craic' of it, but keeps tight hold of the several paper pounds I proffer. He impertinently asks if I am off to see the Wizard? Pretending to be mystified I enquire if he is in, when I am magically informed by the music that he is ...*To the left...to the left...* I mouth back ...*Everything you own in the box to the left...* whilst the Ticket-man reminds me that ...*Don't you ever for a second get to thinking you're irreplaceable?...* We both laugh. He tells me to be on my way with a quip-whip to my hips and lips with the back of his hand and his charming brogue. So it is that we enter the caves and caverns of disco delight.

The Lost and Found Department of Human Hearts re-opens for the night and rudimentary elements of survival in alchemy become essential education in safety. Now queuing at the coat-gatherers dock I watch a Mercy Mission go by, spectacularly dramatic as they lift a collapsed giant into the air and carve a wake through the Sea of Instability and Lake of Lost Souls. *...Oh life...Oh life...* I cannot tell who it is, but as I survey the surrounding scene I can see that all sorts of different folk are in – fairy, hairy, as well as the milling multitudes.

I secure our coat tickets for the night and rearrange my pockets as we head to order drinks. A sexy bear serves in shorts from behind the bar. Our tongues fall out panting with a woof and a grrr! Nods and winks are exchanged; some partly in parody, others with the faint hope of later date action. We leave those downing Stouts and Ales behind, standing at the bar bottoming out on a range of cheap beers whilst we gather water and sundry soft drinks that can be placed in our pockets without spilling. It leaves our arms and hands free to move with the groove.

Our dancing likes to frolic and have fun and can easily absorb and overtake the hiccupping 'hic'-hop factors of the staggering drunk, yet sometimes the Tipsy Monkeys can find more truth! Already beguiled by the boogie, our toes tap and our hips sway in preparation as we wait impatiently in the corridor whilst some of our Mob Squad take an early bathroom break. On their return we turn our attention to the gathering beat and furthering the happiness of our feet. I look for the Host, but no sign of the Holy Ghost yet. Pesky pigeon or diving dove? Either way I am going to "nab him, jab him, tab him, grab him…" even if it turns out to be a more feminine spirit. Does that make me Dick Dastardly or is my Inner Christmas Child just over excitable?

Exploding through doors that swing both ways, the rest of our assorted Bash Street Gang arrive. After high-fives, hugs and hellos all round, we head straight towards the main dance floor – well, straight as we ever can. Momentarily caught in the bottle-necked arches between the designated disco zones several Insinceres pass by in a hurry, double-kissing the air and making quite a show of it, but missing the Heart's mark.

…Shiny happy people laughing…meet me in the crowd, people, people…

Entering into Club Land we push through the ever-changing sea crowd, manoeuvring past the uncomfortable angles of elbows and superficial barbs towards the centre and the softer caress of hips, lips and Cupid's bows. Early limpet love is to be avoided and is frowned upon as much as later, dubious, magnetic mollusc success. We carve a wake through the disco dazed and the generally bemused as we wade onward to the dancing deep.

As mental clarity is not always mine I grasp for the elusive, yet palpable, ethers of the in-between states, neither wet nor dry, by extending my feelings and intuitively connecting the fragmented conditions and situations presented. In the spinning laser beams and mirroring mosaic of glitter balls, smoke and dry ice, it is difficult to see through the surrounding chaos and mists created by our own maya. ...*It's not over yet; it's not over, yeah*... Yet in the Land of Laughter our delusions and illusions are simply fragments of the whole, parts of the All and Everything waiting to be experienced and loved.

On one side of the dance floor the Certainties collect with the Absolutes and the Muscled Marys who swagger with pec-decked attitude, but all are caught in the wave and wash of shared party commonality. The Chubby Bears and Men with Beards and Bellies swell the other shore. Some Lady Boys and Girly Blokes gather with the social Californian and Southern States gals; Lady Bears who push up their hair with one hand whilst clutching their pearls and handbags with the other.

Out on the vast plains of the dance floor, multitudinous creatures abound, some still sulking, stubborn, dull and down-trodden, whilst others sparkle in their free celebration of life's sprawling abundance. Here everyone is a wildebeest free to roam wide in search of Heaven on Earth. Nature is our first God and gets to me every time with its grandeur. The Galapagos speaks and classification begins as a matter of Darwinian bio-faith – observational theories seen and thought, but also felt as esoteric facts.

Apes and bears abound. Baloo slides by followed by the King of the Swingers and some other Hairy VIPs. ...*Mocha chocolate ya ya, creole lady marmalade...* They chase after the Kid with the Creolean Coconuts and his sweet milk, using any excuse to act out the ape. Amongst them, I notice that Mowgli is in and he is all grown up. I feel so proud having watched him progress through the difficult 'coming out' of his teenage years. He is so handsome and has become his own man now, even though he is only aged nineteen.

In the dancing swirl, the puzzles and fruits of Life's evolutionary tree flourish aplenty. I talk to a disenchanted chimp on the end of a splendiferous branch. He is the owner of a golden bough, but does not know it yet. Arms folded, slightly aloof, he will not give in and join the group, not quite yet.

Suspicious and harbouring old hurt as injured discernment, there is still grievance where forgiveness needs to be. I reassure him that we inhabit an Enchanted Kingdom. The thoughtful monkey sees, but does not know how to believe so he hangs round to mimic the other apes, bears and magical creatures to learn from his occasional Wisers.

Born old, he is young and handsome, intelligent and smart, blonde and blue eyed, and knows how to smooth manoeuvre. So ...*It's murder on the dance floor...* as Life eats upon Life, but it does not have to be that way. Competitiveness seemingly opposes cooperation, but not in the new evolution of the Sharing Caring ways. Life in the Super-Duper Universe is good, very good, indeed. Even in the outer fringes of the expanding Cosmos there is scope for All to Love, from the smallest particle (particularly those presently incarnating within the Hydrogen atom) to the biggest, bestest, most magnificent thing. The Physical Universe is a substantially crushing, yet kind, King and Queen. Given time it will bear Pearls from us all.

Swerving around the bend of the mountainous podium, Yogi the Bear makes an appearance and takes a bow. Smarter than the average bear he dances on by in search of Boo Boo in a glorious bow tie, smiling to himself in honour of their special friendship, surreally content and serene. They tie me up in their food questing knots whilst sharing the sandwiches of their recent basket-stealing, picnic capers. Nearby, the newfound joy of a Boy, a Chimp and an Imp two-step in time as a rowdy threesome.

Gruff the big Mountain Gorilla grunts an acknowledgement as he traipses by in the spectral disco mist. Behind him there is a passing parade of assorted animals. For a moment the clogging feet of tap-happy Lancastrian penguins take over until an avuncular Polar Bear distracts them. Thus the Smooth and the Hairy intermingle with one thing in common; they are all in search of fun, fornication and freedom with the big and strong. Aren't we all? Unbutch, but not caring, they watch for some passing beefy biceps from which to hang. They do not struggle with issues of masculinity within sexuality in their feminine pursuit of aesthetic pleasure.

Standing nearby, some Insatiables briskly and rudely fill their dance cards, eyeing up their second and third choices whilst still chatting up their first with thoughts of rutting foremost in their minds. ...*You've got to hold the sucker down*... The Perfunctories prefer to call a shovel a spade and hang around 'good-to-go' just wanting to score. The Dirty Berties flirt with the Men in Uniform whilst the Firemen out hose us all.

…Then if you're tall and handsome and strong…you can wear the uniform and I could play along…

Later on, those in their Bunker Gear will help suds us all down in the roaming foam in semi-sublimated wish fulfilment. Their outfits will fall down alongside the delicious shorts and drop shots of Aussie Rules and Franglais Rugger Buggers like so many torn months from sexy, semi-erotic calendars – forgotten pages and faces as we fumble onto the next in pursuit of athletic perfection and more 'Gods of the Stadium' than we can ever dream of.

…You're such a…you're such a hot temptation, you just walk on in…

Tonight, it would seem, that the Sporty, Handsome and Fit have the mysterious, sought after 'it' in abundance, as do certain attractive individuals – those young, old and devilishly so. The Cheeky Chappies and Mischievous Monkeys have 'it' too, not so much sex appeal, but a merry twinkle in their eye that holds the promise of a potential kiss and a sassy come-on. They are all up for the fun of it. In the renegade company of men, it is not just a matter of aesthetics, but chemistry as well. Thankfully, Bear beauty is very much in the eye of the beholder.

At that moment Hand Lazy Luke and Blubber-the-Bear ride by in the Arkansas Chuggabug waving at us as we watch them pass. We all do the Chattanooga Choo Choo whilst next to us the Slag and Boulder brothers, Fred and Barney, club together banging heads and other parts of their anatomy. For a moment it looks like the Ugs rather than the Jitterbugs seem to have 'it', but all collide in spilling craziness and quickly move on. Even though it is early, some boys and men in the groove around me begin to pull down the Light Divine.

Meanwhile, the Men with Manly, Marvellous Moustaches look magnificent in their evolution of the seventies porn star image. ...*Cuz you're right on time...right on time...* Faded denim and plaid lumberjack shirts still attract from a left over clone scene of yesteryear; a mixture of Village People and residue teenage fantasy. I am full of admiration for the men of muscle (where do they find the time?) but I am Not So Sure, so join up not with the Insecure, but with the Bearded Ladies and Don't Knows; those who are happy finding, exploring, and just being themselves. They are a Creative Crew of Love and Wisdom, accepting who they are and taking others as they find them – the evolutionary resilience of the Experimental Unorthodox.

Some members of our group are unshod Jolly Friars of Olde, dressed in etheric Brown Robes, nearer to Mother Nature than those of the shod

Persecutory Black. No longer cloistered, they now freely climb Life's Vine in merriment and salutations of spiritual friendship. They free the grape and taste the wine, lost in wassailing and fabulous feminine festivities of the now embodied masculine kind. Several house the minds and imaginations of Oxford and Cambridge, yet some of the Wisdoms Seven still reside bone deep, asleep in rose reliquaries. Most sins, though, have been successfully owned, realised and released, whilst others remain fertile fairgrounds of thrilling roustabout activity and clandestine affair.

...Same as it ever was...same as it ever was...time isn't holding us...time isn't after us...

Beliefs, desires and feelings, by their watery flowing nature, are closer to our bodies and God than airy thoughts, so it is through their ambiguous flow that I experience kindness and the individual me through the group soul of those gathered about. Me? I am in disguise, yet unravelling – an ordinary man of mystery in search of a true, yet ever changing, identity. I know I will have to travel down long, lost lanes, fly across far, flung fields and soar above salt-scented seas to find and release my inner, elusive, dancing chameleon. Even dancing indoors I can feel the breeze and the surf breaking about me.

...Ha ha ha...hee hee hee...I'm a laughing gnome and you can't catch me...

In crossing the cosmos tonight in pursuit of finding my Divine Child and Inner Creature, I hope I can survive the journeying and make it back in one piece. All I have to do is shake myself out, let go of all the injuries and experiences of the adult me, and dance through the protecting, purifying fire. Simple really, the only thing is that I seem to have lost the Map of Me in my current mix of inner joy and outer uncertainty. …*Cause I gotta have faith, faith, faith*… Yet what kind of satisfaction am I truly in search of this evening?

Feathers up, ruffles out, some passing Peacocks and dithering Dandies stand on parade in the walkway seemingly unafraid as a series of Spites, Spats and Spitfires fly by, gunning for fights and hopes of revenge. In their gobby cackle and infernal noise I notice some Unsilent Screamers and Uncracked Tough Nuts, hard and unpicked, rubbing up against each other. …*You said you loved me, but that was just a lie, just a lie*… Untender tinder and friction is everywhere.

Some of the Rough Fucks do not know where use stops and abuse starts with their in-your-face jabbing and narcissistic ways. The lack of respect is repellent, but they allow a boundary affirming 'fuck off' to be said with pleasure and they never take it personally, worst luck. Yet ripeness is present here tonight with the inclusion of the Mellow, Soft and

Lovely, unfortunately their more mature reality is often tinged with some sadness too.

…Please, Mr, please, don't play B-17…it was our song, it was his song, but it's over…

Peering into mirrored surfaces, the Peter Perfects and Penelope Pitstops are in with their accumulated weekly emotional journeys and sexual perils. They are pretenders all, some super-pleased with self, preened, pressed and spotless, with their constant invitations to each other to almost get married; yet they never will. The fun is in the pursuit and the trying; that and the applying of lipstick and maquillage, but at least they know that, right? Well, I hope they do.

In the crowd Pig-Toads, Wobbly Walruses and Love Hounds throng and prosper. They are all up for the hits and misses of cartoon kisses, and on nights such as these anything can happen including that rarest of transformations into the most charming of princes. The Tweedledees run around with the Tweedledums tying themselves up in slapstick moments as they bumble around trying to sort themselves out.

Similarly, some other duos and trios will wind us up all night in their old black-and-white film comedy capers, dashing around chasing each other. With their accidents and near misses, they let the ridiculousness shine through again and remind us all of the haphazard, chance-encounter nature of living. Only connect, but we already are. ...*You got a different point of view...* Is it beautiful?

In the far corners of the room some Bull Roarers – those grown-up children Orphaned, Abandoned or Lost in the Rushes so long ago – gather together trying to sympathise and make it better. They hang out with the slick Jets, Sharks and Water Babies. Blancmange Bob in his rubber trunks swims in the shadows whilst bouncing around the edges of the disco bowl having underwear fun. He is wobbly and knows how to entertain.

In the shallows, fins out, all manner of exotic fish folk fluster by. Some flap excitedly, whilst others are caught on the flail and flounder in the hop and flop of the party flow. Submerged in drowning sound and spinning light, it is like being in a beautiful briny ballroom in an underwater world. Prawn-like, most of those on the dance floor do the conventionally limited sashimi shuffle. I mentally note that I must find some more exciting electric eels to wiggle and conga with later.

Nearby, the Captivating Young and the Tall Haughty Taughty stand by ready to ensnare, mouths and arms snapping shut like Venus Fly Traps on passing juicy morsels. With their square chins and slightly cold eyes they are attractive, but too aloof for my liking. Hardly the type sought by the interactive E-computer sons of the X-generation whose thoughts of waking up next to a beautiful communicative man has become Everyone's collective dream.

...Fifteen minutes with you...well, I wouldn't say no...people see no worth in you...oh but I do...

Dating and mating has to be a job of enthusiastic reciprocity and mutual give and take, or you are in for a lazy, bad time. Unless, that is, you like them to lay back selfishly thinking of England or you harbour gay boy fantasies of working hard to silently turn a straight man gay for the night. Yet some think they would, think they could, given half the chance, and of course it is always worth the trying. Those involved eat with their eyes and think about some hard wooing.

Several Leeches are in acting like bloodsuckers are wont to do, clinging and draining, hanging around Mister Look-Don't-Touch who loses so much, but is happy enough in his splendid isolation. He is busy attracting and repelling with his muscles and tan, wearing trendy sunglasses indoors and a designer torn cowboy top with a tall Stetson hat. In his mind he is covered in 'rhinestones' and keeps himself busy being as unavailable as a celebrity Super Porn Star can be. He lets me dance with him and I am left feeling that somehow it has been my privilege.

...Nice guys get washed away like the snow and the rain, there's...a load of compromisin', on the road to my horizon...

Much more entertaining are the congregating Cow Girls and Silly Moos with their swinging udders, farts and earthy ways. They are all hilarious birds having fun in sexual blue jeans with no care for penance. Jezebel is in, a greedy girl when she should be generous, hanging out with the former High Sex Priestesses and Nuns-on-the-Run from convent living. They are all working girls now who know the worth of their marmalade and other honey stuff.

...My milk shake is better than yours, I could teach ya, but I'd have to charge...

Not as humble as Hamble or sweet as Fruit Pie, Jezebel is unsure if she is a Holy Whore anymore. It is rumoured that the peroxide twins, Celebrity and Glamour, brought about her downfall. They captured it all on videotape; chastity belts, slings and VD number 8, then Youtubed it. The Pox, how vile! Of them, that is. Twisted Sisters and Nasty Girls all!

...I won't give in...I won't feel guilty...rant and rave to manipulate me...from the nipple to the bottle never satisfied...

Our friend Samantha, black as velvet and wonderful as sin wrapped in chocolate, has never forgiven them. She sells her wares and lollipops in the gentleman's toilet, up to her elbows in Chupa Chups and adult babies screaming or lost in the sucking on the lobes of her ears. She sells scents at one pound a spray and makes you feel nice. Pay for one and she will secretly pray for you too for she has the Midnight Power. The secret? Her soul is already saved in the caring of others. That and a pinch of voodoo.

On the dance floor, the Archetypes and Stereotypicals lurch about having fun. The Hots and the Hot 'n' Tots, and those that are not, and those that can go and rot, join up with the Just Lusts and the few Juicy Lucys of pneumatic proportions that are left able to stagger and dance. Some have lips that kiss like camels even though they wear charming, cherry-flavoured chap stick. Yet the Imperious Cock and Biting Vagina will not hold sway here tonight. Apart from the Big Ridge itself, the Rigidities must go. Spittoon theories of love will fade into *...Sexual healing...oh when I get this feeling I need sexual healing...sexual healing is good for me...* and we all need that.

Affectionate by nature, I am on the soft and gentle side of love and touch, evolving that which can lead to beatitude like Thai sweet fusion, flowering orchids and soldiers' weaponry melting into the arms of their lovers, paid or not. Does it always have to be about the bayonet? What about the pierced? In our abiding passion where lies the wound and where the agony? How long is the journey belonging to Love's healing and soul recovery? Dancing next to me some Anguished – those torn between two lovers – divide and suffer in the flames of their Heart. I wish them whole again, one heart, one mind, but I cannot take away their pain.

...Do it! Do it! Do the Hustle!...

Personally, the Sensualists have it over the Bone Breakers and Bruisers tonight, although right now everyone does the obligatory 'hustle' until decision time takes over. I out gristle the El Gringos in this regard and remind them all that they will share flowers and soft kisses again. Just close your eyes and freely take one. The Romantics have it in a single caress whilst the Teenagers, and those in their Twenties, rave and rage having it in hormonal tons. They execute their embraces with exuberant snogs and French kisses behind the bike sheds, between the arches, and in the smoking garden. A few of the older ones still have it in undeniable Spunky Daddy energy.

...Release me, release my body, set me free...

So the evening will slowly become all about journeys of dance, sex, fun and exhaustion. Sublimation, mutual shagability and morning after satisfaction are all at stake as strange demonstrations of human erotic desire are displayed like Birds of

Paradise before bedding down for the night. Everything is possible in the promise of a stranger's twinkling eye, flashing smile or upturned feather. Start from a point of abundance and you will leave laughing and dancing on a high; start from a point of lack and you will be dealing with the blind desires and disappointment of others, including the frustration of your own flesh. I align myself accordingly.

Nearby, some Teases ease their titillation with spittle on their lips trying it on with the far away Fantasists. ...*Stand and deliver your money or your life...* Some realities were made to clash. In quick procession some annoying, artificial Hi-Bye's fly by trying to usurp our territory, so I up elbows and counter their attack. In a second wave, those with forked tongues breed suspicion and envy as they insult on the assault. Their poisonous gossip and confetti-carving confessions suddenly strew an infected dance floor, so in rebuff I deliver some unkind, grounded realities.

...You've been telling me lies...

I do not think they will be thanking me just yet as home truths, particularly those without kindness, have it over accusations and snide allegations if only for a short while. True talk on the dance floor is only for those limited few that can manage sincerity and some form of honest consciousness. ...*Hey, the lights are on, but there's no-one home...* This is not a privilege, merely an unfortunate fact for the Grown Up, the Cold Stone Sobers and those few inhabiting the Corners of the Aware Mind.

Those sarcastically inclined revellers that briefly surround pointedly lip-synch, mocking me, whilst mindlessly mouthing some words *...Hung up on you...* Maturely, I prove to them that this is not so by inanely miming the placing of a telephone receiver down and turning my back. Cold shoulders are raised all round to freeze me out. Moments turn to minutes before they are bored and realise that there are more important people to impress and annoy. Inwardly, I thank god that they have gone.

My personal Mc'Gyptian high security is usually present to defend me from the Pricks, Dicks and Don't Cares, but he is currently busy running a hundred errands and holding a life together. Nearby is one of the stately Flint Kings of Kent, the politics of courts still upper most in his mind, but with an etiquette and education for those that forget politeness. *...What about me?...* He looks over, rolls his eyes at the antics of others and mimes a scene involving a typewriter and the state of my brain. He knows I am thinking when I ought to be dancing.

I get a fit of the girly giggles. I am so in love with my friends and Life's mind-boggling mess that I end up doubled-over, laughing and laughing until my sides ache and my eyes water. *...It's all about you...* Apparently! Just when I thought Life might, for a moment, begin to be about me. Luckily, the Smiler within is now firmly fixed in like the grin on a perma-win of a slot machine. Jackpot! Yet what to do with all the descending, whirling threads of cosmic gold and colour?

Spinning around like sugar floss in a candy machine, unconditionally pink, fluffy and full of childish pleasure, I turn about myself and notice the soft and gentle delights of a nearby Koala, a Kanga and a Russkie Bear dancing together. A Joker and a mad King Penguin waddle by. You see, we are all just God's bundles of fun, creatures of whim and caprice, dancing alongside each other, trying to get along. The assorted individuals all form a circle, hands holding shoulders, and pass cheeky kisses along the line before slumping into a group love-hug.

...I knock on wood, baby...oh oh oh oh oh...

My Puck self takes a bow and looks to the surrounding Sexuals and Star-Crossed Lovers. Love lines, previously laid down for the journeying million miles, are being experienced in the here and now of the myriad lives that are ours. Not up for procreation in this life (I am all for adoption and fostering), it only leaves dance and sex for pleasure and spiritual liberation. Yet 'Mok'sha' is not for the faint hearted. I need to find my inner Dancing Warrior to help achieve that.

Others have a more serious approach and agenda to the evening ahead, but tonight I am on the fun and playful side of a good night out. This means I can go anywhere and the evening can lead to Magic if I but let it. Not everyone wants to go there for it means that you have to return to that which you never left and change, however incrementally, the imagined self living within the Dream. The parting old medium's words come back to haunt me:

"Remember in this life," she said sweetly, "To love wisely, not too well."

Of all the things to tell me it is a most difficult reminder and ask. It is as bad as telling a boy with itchy, musical feet to sit still and study. So far I can only think of 5 wise things I have done in my life, all of them involve leaving, following the heart and acts of brave faith. As I continue to walk through the chaos of the Western World, its people and the strange situations I meet, the Spaghetti Gods – Good, Bad and Ugly – seem to be in constant operation causing confusion in so many peoples' lives. I let those Gods of Misunderstanding know that at last I realise that Love is the answer, so what questions of Mind can possibly remain?

...When the heartache is over...

Issues of past relationships briefly arise. I am easy-going, but somehow difficult and relating has not always gone smoothly as my identity has grown and changed. Love certainly gives and takes – was my heart, for them, just a demo? All my life I have been a square peg in a round hole, yet tonight I take my new coordinates from Tintin and the Doctor's Time Machine, which likewise has a 'chameleon circuit'. The Who of that Growing Self is only one brother of the W's 5 of investigative journalism. What, Where, When and Why stand by rubbing shoulders with the almost twins – the Brothers Grimm, not Thompson. Aye, there lies the prism rub of it! For my indie perception-conception is all to do with the strange workings of my Mind's light and shadow, yet through the years and tears my Heart is slowly taking the lead.

...I guess that's nothing new...'cause when you meet someone who doesn't follow all the rules...it changes ev'rything you do...'cause you've got love, love, love on your side...

Nearby I hear the distracting sound of spurs jingling as the Lawful and the Outlawed swing through the disco saloon doors all buckles, belts and cheek-revealing chaps. Cowboys and Indians, Angels and Demons, have all dressed up to come and play, acting out their cameo roles in this purported last dance of mine. Me, I am dressed as a Casual Lone

Star drifter, wandering where the need takes me in the Three Stetson Saloon of Life. I carry a gun that I will hopefully never have to use at the ready, but in these shifting, dangerous days we all have to beware the rattlesnakes.

...Her heart's like crazy paving, upside down and back to front, she says ooh, it's so hard to love when love was your great disappointment...

As my personal dancing joy becomes firmly affixed I smile contentedly, trying to ignore all the outward forces – the issues and tissues of other people as well as Life's more personal conflicts – that vie for attention. However, I notice amongst the Christmas Cowboy Crowd that the Mighty Power Penis Ranger is in, a thickset, muscular sexual synthesiser of a man, as strong as a Shire horse. He holds me from behind and I let him hug me, secretly pleased. I press against the front of his tree-trunk legs whilst reaching back with both my arms around his waist, rancher style.

Suddenly, I am sitting in front, astride a fast horse, galloping across the prairie plans with a Marlborough Man on a demi-semi bucking bronco. Sexual ecstasy runs away with me like rivulets streaming into immersing desire. I wonder how it would feel to be with him. *...I would give you my finest hour, the one I spent watching you shower...* Bursting at the jean seams, I find myself tossed up on the horns of the Red Goat God, rodeo-style.

The Power Ranger is good, but the sublimated moment is passing and more underlying vanilla than expected, yet he undoubtedly occupies a Master's role. He will be your fantasy for a while, at least until the song expires, and then he will leave you. Thus left, you will be dealing with a new set of truths if you believed any of it to be real. He is very Professional, but asks of us a question: would we ever enter into any relationship unless we fooled ourselves with fantasy first?

Meanwhile, I simply pretend I am having horror and fun, masking my true emotions and motivations until their unravelling end. I run through all the many permutations and variations with him until eventually I unfold myself into the maturing aspects of the more masculine me. We would be oaks together if we were trees. In growing, rooted realisation I am reminded of that wonderful Russian saying: "Love is blind, but sees from far away".

Around us, other Sexy Daddies, Silver Foxes and Papa Smurfs linger about getting serious. It is a chance for some to play with the Big Boys, but it begins to dawn on me that I am slowly becoming one of them. Unlike Canadian hustlers I only dance the one dance, one song long, whether with friends or strangers, however hairy-the-hunk or likeable-the-lad is. I do not charge, but I wonder if circumstances were different or bags of money were involved, what I would do? Sex, for some, is both Nature's calling and credit card.

Out of nowhere I find I am suddenly fighting Viking with Thorson, Olaf and Noggin the Nog. Tall, bearded, red-headed, it is a mighty Scandinavian invasion as they pick me up of my feet and pass me around their group, laughing. Hovering a foot above the floor I espy their Ice Dragon, Groliffe, Keeper of Treasures, asleep in a cold cave in the Glass Mountains. I do not wake him for I am in need of something warmer tonight.

As if on command Idris the Dragon enters, friend of Ivor and Bani Moukerjee; the tonal Welsh who like to do what they want to do, disliking the timetables of too much work for where is the magic in that? Their hills are alive with so much music for a reason, you know, Boy'o. Idris sleeps in the engine, but in rousing stokes the train's fires and tilts the pelvic bowl. Something is rising within as three pipe-organ whistles give off steam. Is it simply childish delight or is it something more serious hidden inside that begins to frighten and stir? The Vikings leave with pillaging on their mind. They are not in avoidance of adult energies.

During this melee I sense the wanting of some Hungry Holes looking on, watching us dance as the snakes and chains of their jealousy writhe around their corpulent bodies. The serpents of envy stare into my face, spitting. I seek advice. Even though I am momentarily scared by their blatancy, I look them in the eye and call them out. I come armed with an esoteric knife and antidotes for such poison.

Permission seeking turns to permission giving in this Shaman's urban journey of the reconstituted Tribal Self. So I cut through their mean-spirited coils and throw away their offering of miserable roses to let the new wood bloom through. I could, of course, just laugh, for devils – although they enjoy dancing – do not like that. As one of the late night clan of Love Cats, I find I can out contraire the contraries and other Marys any day. It is not a quality I am very pleased about, but somehow I am very good at it.

...We're so wonderfully, wonderfully, wonderfully, wonderfully pretty!...

Mapping sexuality on the mathematical graph between the X and Y-axis, the Versatile play a ratio waiting game, balancing the equations between Top and Bottom. Genetic X and Y factors figure, particularly those caught up in the XXY gene configuration. The Actives and Passives are ever present, the latter outnumbering the former four to one. ...*When love takes over*... Subs and Doms confuse. The Lazy Butts and Can't-Be-Arsed drift aimlessly, attracted to the Seemingly Handsome and Seriously Sexy but getting short shrift.

The Implausible run around in pursuit of the Impossible, chasing their teenaged butts with T-shirts bunched behind like frisky ponytails. Some are annoyingly cute. The Plausible and the Possible chat and feel each other up at the bar in handfuls of reality before passing into the Shadow Lounge – the Room of No Names – where in private, yet semi-public for the voyeuristic few, it is mating without dating. It is sex for casual sex's sake; call it Universal Love on a nightly basis if you will, procurement if you must. Some are in pursuit of a promise, whilst others are eager to forget the pain of the last in the hands of the next.

...It's gotta be big...honey bring it close to my lips...

In need of company a hard rising becomes an expression of self that craves the sharing of skin. Desire left unexpressed can become repressed desperation – unchecked it becomes libidinous and lustful. For a few it can be a killing concern, for others just fun. Oral, as well as other non-verbal types of communication, make men feel alive even if only for the moment.

In the club's shady pools and shadow places, the Unconventionally Handsome hang around doggedly. Loitering in between the wet and dry states, they understand the true glory that such hollows, holes and dim spaces afford. A darkened room becomes an alley or a two-way street where parked strangers meet. For some it is a platform for love, trains in the passing, a court and shunt, then a quick sparking.

Moans and groans are rapidly followed by a handful of grateful release. Sparkling in this way is a momentary ending of pent-up sexual tension and solitariness, before the next wave builds. Music drifts through as doors open... ...*A little more love, a little more peace...* ...and shut. Sex is, after all, an altered state and there is magic in the masturbatory and touching arts.

...Relax, don't do it, when you want to go to it...got to hit me, hit me, hit me with those laser beams...

The Horizontal and Vertical Rays hold the answer; lay lines of penetrative and receptive light behind the scenes, yet who biologically is helped by the physics of that? Plasma fusion and auric explosion are all part of the cosmic order and dynamic, but instinctive touch is still the best human spark of all. On a bed, floor or up against a wall is the only other way I can put it or that it can be put.

…You can have it with a buzz, you can have it with a ring, and if you really want it you can have a ding-a-ling…

Outside the Room of No Shame, the Tran and Poly Sexuals float by, laughing at my lessons and caution for they are free from it all. The Been-There-Done-That have been there and done that, wearing it on their skin like some fabulous T-shirt and newly designed attitude tattoo. There is no one logo of lust suitable for me. Unlike others, their Liberated Selves seek the light, shun the dark and let it all hang out. I sometimes wish they did not, but good for them. Unblushable, they truly seem to be without shame.

A few new Asymmetrics wander around after them, strange looking, falsely untroubled young souls to my aging eyes. Near-by, and closer to my heart, the Polynesian flame-flowers of Old Oceania open up – orange, gold and red – to reveal the sensual and sexual life of tribal people and tropical plants. Their South Pacific breezes reach me, blowing pollen across golden skies and honeyed skin. They remind me of the positive/negative charges of an ever-changing soul-sex state.

Inside, my Anima and Animus sympathetically rise up like twin-headed serpents, unseen together since teenage years. The Laws of Attraction and Repulsion are in operation as the emotional bi-sexuality of feeling allows us to relate to the 'All of

Life' in their constant flux and flow. This means that the second glances will get their chances and there is hope for us all in this brief evolutionary moment on Earth that we are temporarily given. Tonight, I feel, anything goes.

A nearby Ancient Androgyne helps me recall those past times when the fertile promiscuity of polarised pseudopodia and simple plasma-pods reigned, long before invented, separated notions of the masculine/feminine divide. In present existence those rare Androgynous are too few in number for most to remember or know how to relate to. These Primordial Ones can feel so old and alone that I always smile to show that I empathise and understand, but they too must move on within the present evolutionary cycle of planetary love. If I, an Ethereal, can do it, so can they.

Several former Pagans, Primitives and a Druid King, once head splitters all, dance around the Ancient One in endless spirals of stone and chalk circles whilst chanting his pain away like good Buddhist monks so often do. Such lyrical acts of kindness and generosity help us all to get along whether we are waving, drowning, or simply bopping away to a popular song. You see, swimming in the Sea of Cosmic Consciousness, we are all in this together.

As I nod in awe of the DNA shuffle, my altered state changes to become aware of the Venusians and members of the other floating, gaseous worlds. A group of Morphines and Anaesthetists waft through remembering the amusement of Edwardian parties and Victorian parlour gas games, with their squeaky balloons and helium laughing. Some of those who have ridden the dragon have Opium snakes attached which lie sideways, totally lost and aurically trailing, yet still they tug trying to escape to explore the astral planes. To them, desire is everything.

Drifting by in a mist, they leave a faint odour of room aromas behind them, which attracts a few Hover Flies, momentary mates in the near end-of-year fun. As they disperse their cheap perfume brings me back down to Earth just in time to notice a Parade of Poufs teeter by. Cha Cha clicks her heels in a Cuban way as the Slipper of Venezuela fans her feathers and milks her entrance for more than it is worth. Mademoiselle 'Croque' Monsieur and Ruby Two Shoes shimmy past in their matching red sequined dresses. Lalique follows on behind. They all look like tassels and baubles torn from a fake Fabergé tree.

Laughing, the Nasty Pigs stand around in buckled harnesses and assorted rubber to watch one of them fall. For them there is nothing funnier than a camp man in drag and make-up go sprawling. The Butch and the Fems can be like that sometimes, at odds with one another. It is all leather or feather with them.

…Let's get down…let's get down, down, down…

The fallen Lalique picks himself, and the contents of his clutch bag, up. Those in frumpy drag and sensible shoes help him back up onto his horribly high platforms. The Drag Queens look down at his knees and torn 'American Tan' tights in dismay. Nail lacquer will soon stop that hole from laddering, but no-one has the right colour. They become busy all of a fuss and a fright; a gaggle and cackle of gays in a wonderful primping.

Without the aid of a mirror, Wardrobe Mistress Quickly smooths Lalique's hairpiece and checks his outfit. Lalique dusts himself down, cussing the cow that pushed him. 'Outrage!' Quicker than spleen, brighter than bile, he knows all the rapid tart retorts for he has been on the floor before. I pity the person on the sharp end of a drag queen's tongue or riotous stiletto. *…Glad tidings of comfort and joy, comfort and joy…* but I thank them all for Stonewall.

So it is that all the Dirty Princesses and Hog Monsters have come to the mud hollow to enjoy the post-Christmas, retro-express Hustler's Ball. The

Woofs and Grrs accidentally bump and grind together trading meat – young, middle-aged and horse – whilst slinging their hooks. The predator-prey relationship is always close to the surface in the hunt for happiness. The disciplined S&M-er's look on with horror at the Camp-as-Christmases who suddenly descend with their alluring tinsel and vulgar frivolities, which sparkle and catch the light. ... *Your disco, your disco...*

Glittering and shiny, those Camp-as-Christmas, Glad Rags and Glitzy Handbags act as reminders that truly, madly, deeply, our disco does indeed need us, although they would capsize us all in their shimmying 'she-sayings' and popcorn ways. Baffled by their quick passing magical moonbeams, my Sacred Creature roams but always returns to smile at me all love, madness and compassion. Part English Rose and part British Bull Dog in the blending, he has the most wonderfully expressive eyes that beguile like a child.

I return the spell that he placed on me – one of healing, love and infinite blessings given through trust so many eons ago. He loves me so much, and I him, but I can get lost in the overwhelming experience of it all and in the fear of the here-and-now. Sometimes I push and resist, but in those moments he pulls me on. *...Honey honey, how you thrill me, ah-hah, honey honey...* I thank God that he does. Do I do the same for him? I fervently hope so, but he is so much more fun whilst I am so simply and easily led on.

Games of Follow My Leader have turned into Hide and Seek throughout Time. Yet somehow we find each other over and over again. Luckily I am heat seeking and my Beloved is just the right temperature to end all my suffering. …*Honey honey, nearly kill me, ah-hah, honey honey*… His Buddhist monk lifted me off my cross many years ago and I am just learning how to catch up. He is my Windy Miller and Aloysius Bear All-in-One. To us is given the strangest, yet most wonderful, of journeys – the Two of Cups and entwining Tarot Lovers. I know him from a thousand lives past where we have lived together as brothers. We have saved and killed each other so many times.

My Beloved is loved by everybody and is his own exasperating, unstoppable free agent. Compared to him, I feel like Mrs Kinsey, less a sexual radical, but open to occasional offers of free mating with love. I am particularly attracted to the unconventional artistic and creative, the conventional handsome and sexy, and the progressive sensual and strong; all those that have found themselves interested in Life's universal learning. Libidos and luck might lessen with age, yet opportunity and chance remain fine things, and if Fortune permits I try to take full, but fair, advantage of any situation!

...And now I know what they mean, you're a love machine...oh, you make me dizzy...

Even in my late-teenage recklessness of the now middle-aged, masculine revelling kind, a fusty part of me still remains on the shelf waiting to be dusted off. Yet for whom and for what am I waiting? Slowly, steadily, I find myself slipping towards the state of Gay Abandonment and Letting Go that belongs with being away with the fairies and blissfully entrapped in God's sweet coma of momentary forgetfulness. There goes the last of my grey. Here comes my rainbow heart, feet and fingers. I dance on, up and over the White Cliffs of Dover to where the occasional Bluebirds of Happiness fly.

...Oh, my love...a million days in your arms is never too much...I just don't wanna stop...too much, never too much...

In the lifting haze some boys with poi's swing into late night action and an assortment of Mr Men walk by. Mr Happy, Mr Silly and Mr Daydream drift alongside one of the whizzing Little Misses. She is hyper-organised whilst coming to grips with Mr Messy. Meanwhile, Mr Ditsy and Mr Toppy upturn Master Bates and the other members of Pugwash's seamen crew in the chaos of their sea-faring ways. They are usually in pursuit of a handsome cabin boy or two, but the rugged-looking Captains, Haddock and Birdseye, fare better on their own.

Nearby, the blissful, burbling, babble of babies emanates around us: Urgle, Burgle, Bungle, Boing and Bounce all joyously pounce and descend upon us in a shambolic group meeting and greeting. After one giant, enfolding hold and mother-of-all-hugs a reciprocating, exuberant burp is released then we know *'It's time…for a story.'* Our old friends Happiness and Laughter are here as the very silly and the wonderfully annoying take over.

Hartley the mad-march hare and all those from high above the Rainbow call out to us and wave. Excitedly, we wave back. Tog, the Pogles, and Paulus the little wood gnome wander out of the Enchanted Woods. Spotty Dog and The Hundred Acre Gang appear. Even Andy, Teddy and Loopy Lou have come out to play as baskets open and urban grown-ups roam back into the wilds of childhood.

Thus encouraged, I unleash my creatures, my dogs and cats, and let the animals out as I honour the instinctual – the sex, love and savagery that have brought us brave soldiers back here on our current Gaia mission. This is no Lord of the Flies escapade, yet it is no Muppet mission either. My ghostly friend Mr Ben appears and disappears as if by magic on another excellent adventure. Never mind! I am sure he will return later. The doors on changing rooms, like closets and wardrobes, have a habit of unexpectedly opening and closing, yet not all swing both ways and love sent is not always returned.

Meanwhile, the nearby Broken and Lost Boys look poetic and distant as beautiful, sad young men are inclined to do. They are romantically engaged in the tragedy of the losing lessons of the Lonely Heart of the Early Twenties. There are those who leave and those who are left. As you grow older you realise that the roles of 'Heart Breaker' and 'Heart Broken' are equally difficult to play. In order to gain Peace we have to come to terms with them both.

...Why does my heart feel so bad?...why does my soul feel so bad?...

Weary of the emptiness, some Lonesomes sit on the surrounding sofas sharing conversations and consolations, whilst others go outside to smoke. A few standing Sensibles peruse the mad dancing throng from the outside edges and quieter shores, smiling to themselves, content to watch and condemn. Some are Seasoned Souls trying not to look too bored, having to engage with the social scene whilst not really wanting to bother. Yet still, it might offer an antidote to their occasional loneliness.

...If that's all there is my friends, then let's keep dancing, let's break out the booze and have a ball, is that all there is?...

Good humour balances precariously on top of a wave, a musical crest waiting to crash and spill upon us all. Around us the Accords, Cadences and Discords gather; so too the Austeres and New Puritans casting their beady eyes over our friends, the Tattooed Taboos. The Trials and Tribulations watch on like thorny opportunists awaiting their chance for a cheap shot. ...*Take me home...I'm in Heaven...seems like Heaven, so much in Heaven...* In my current state of awareness, I have to out-dance them all.

Crossing to an open space in a desperate bid to move and extend my arms, I see in a wink of a man's twinkling eye that the Cock Sucking Sons of Bastards are in, including Colorado Joe, everybody's friend. All the Singing Brothers of the heavenly sent Sevenths are here to hoedown, toe to heel, in lines and reels. How fantastic! In search of brides and husbands, the wisecracking Stud Muffins stand by watching, licking their lips and snaking their hips in anticipation of enchantment and its eating. They pass their illicit fruit with mouthfuls of kisses, but love themselves more than others. For them, sin is but a centuries-old trademark, just the church's mainstay meaning of the eating of apples. What a logo! Is it ours?

...Meeting Mr Right, the man of my dreams...

Love-sexy is simply the egotistical way of things when you are that much of a Horn-Dog and have the assurance of youth on your side. Innocence crumbles under the penetrating nature of experience. It will be re-gained in loving honesty. ...*finally you've come along*... Sexual confidence is everything here. Knowing who you are and what you want are important signallers. It is the Middle Aged Muttons who are old before their time that better watch out. "Act your age, not your shoe size," unless Disgrace be thy name. Thus cursed, we set out to do our worst!

...finally it has happened to me...

Personally, I am more interested in bouncing off the walls like a Pinball Kid, but it is early yet and we have only just started. There is a long evening ahead and I know it is all in the pacing for a successful mission and a good night out. I feel like a boy in a bubble dancing inside a walled and secret garden, which only now is slowly becoming an enchanted kingdom. Both bubble and wall must go, but it scares me so and I do not know how to let them fall. You see, the illusion of separateness is sometimes still mine as I whirr around my hamster wheel believing I can achieve Heaven on my own. It is not so.

In the greater scheme of things there is no me, only us, and I have to trust in the Guiding Hand and my dancing friends to help me on. I forget that the Overseeing Angels and Spiritual Masters rejoice and root for us, but I cannot rush the Unfolding or the

Unveiling. I have desire to push the wall down quickly, but Patience and Prudence are task-asking, brick-removing teachers that I try to tackle to the ground. It is so frustrating playing their waiting game.

I know I must not hold back the Sharing, yet however close, the time of Flowering, Ripening and Picking is not in my hands. The great spiritual Gardener and Farmer in the sky are responsible for the coordinated shaking and harvesting. Yet who am I in this New Awakening? ...*You ain't seen the best of me yet*... Are we all just beings of emanating light running back to the feet of God? Can I really dance through air without a care? I hear the whoosh of wings – are there angels passing by?

Meanwhile, Billy the Best Disco Kid in Town arrives to join the party. Another giant of a man with the kindest heart and a reminder that really, it is only another night out with the lads, ten lords a-leaping, and a disco waiting to be danced. I mean to say that we are out clubbing again joined at the beat in search of kicks, kinks and Peter Pan; London South somewhere across a car park, former forbidden fruit dancing under a railway arch which acts as a protective rainbow.

Around me, the mass-produced, fast-living, modern-day X-Factor Stars and Wanna-Be's enter Spangle Land. Yet I have already left their Kansas far behind me, Toto too, as I come ever closer to a conscious, childhood, spiritual state. Stripped down essentials and simple bare necessities are all that are required, for Soul and Grace live here in wonderment and purity.

...Sweet dreams are made of this, who am I to disagree? I travel the world and the seven seas...everybody's looking for something...

Sometimes we have to go back to be able to move forward. As I leave one current reality for another, I am caught within a beautifully colourful state where remembrances of the far away and long ago collide in kaleidoscopic vision like tumbling, brightly coloured beads. Awareness of the surrounding music momentarily fades and I am suddenly back at the old family home. In the garden, my brothers and I limbo under hung washing, flying with outstretched arms through big white sheets pegged out on the line. We chase each other as we explore the interlinking gardens, streets and open spaces at our resourceful fingertips – portals into Nature's Great Outdoors and our fertile imaginations.

Taking to our skates and skateboards, various pogo sticks, stilts and space hoppers, we spill excitably onto the pavements. Knights of the Tracks Scalextric collide with Evil Knievel; Dare Devil and Spiderman swing through the streets on improvised slinky springs. As part of 'Action Man patrol' we all 'fall in!' whilst others become bionic. We take to our bikes and scampering feet to roam the farms, the parks and recreational grounds. We scrape our knees falling from trees as we go scrumping. We climb the caves and rocks to see what adventures we can find by the sea and the sand, running about on high cliff land like kites in the wind. Playing out is best, however much we annoy the neighbours.

As I wander the fields of my ancestral past, the images and echoes of my early years are surrounded by the sound of incessant gulls cawing in the sky, whilst the sounds of distant breaking surf fills my shell-like ear. I can still hear the distant mer-worlds calling to me. I would live under water in aquamarine caves if I could. Well, with Marina, Captain Troy Tempest and his team of aquanauts to keep me company in the colourful adventures of Stingray.

Running indoors, I am standing on a chair at the kitchen table helping my Mother to bake. We are having fun making cakes for all the family. I am stirring the spoon and eating the left-over mix scraped from the bottom of the bowl in sugar-rush Heaven. The radio is on, as always, rocking its rhythms of popular ease. I dance around the room. In between the supervised folding of laundry and coupling of socks we play cards. Single combinations first, then snap and pairs.

I take to reading like a fish to water. Books become rainbow bridges taking me on extraordinary journeys. A simple turn of the page and a shake of the snow globe shift me to Scandinavia where the Finn Family Moomintrolls take over: Mamma and Pappa, Snufkin and Sniff, and the ever-elusive Snork Maiden. Stories are tales of travel with inviting worlds to visit. Tucked up in bed I read voraciously consuming words like a hungry bird pecking at juicy worms.

Momentarily in my mind, my former child's life turns into a big band TV sentimental journey, so I turn the dial and tune back in. Memories of childhood entertainment swell on the offing, flying as though they are alive. As the Telescope-of-Time flips about itself and turns to view distant events I am further diminished. I grow younger, littler, and I am back sitting on the living-room floor 'Watching with Mother' the wondrous TV.

The Amazed Child is here. Small and Tiny from The Clangers peer over the edge of a passing Cloud, mesmerised as they gaze up at musical raindrops and a Top Hat full of ribbetting frogs. Escaping from moonscapes I tell the Magic Box that is not Bud the Florist nor Policeman Plod, but Alberto Frog and his Amazing Animal Band! A pinch of The Herbs floats by. Parsley, the loveable green lion, is here. How we still love him.

"Herbidacious!"

The Keeper of the magic word speaks and inner doors fly open. As I cross the Threshold everyone becomes a Zebedee in *Le Manège Enchanté*; a delightful world of dogs, cows, rabbits and snails, girls, boys and musical roundabouts. Boing means bedtime for them, but not for me as beautiful ZaZa, busybody Kiki and loveable old Hector all wave hello. Up to their old tricks they will all help me keep awake through the encroaching sleep state.

A golden haloed Tweetie-Pie flits by pursued as ever by that big-old, bad-old Puddycat. Dogtanian and some swashbuckling Muskahounds leap into action as a mild-mannered janitor materialises to practise his martial art moves. Hong Kong Phooey now hovers like a guardian angel to the right of me, keeping me safe on my trance-dance journey through the dark of night. To the left of me, escaping from the back of the Mystery Machine, Scooby Doo and Shaggy too are now present, scoffing snacks, but cheering me on through several, badly-masked demons and villains.

Behind me some top dogs, TCs and assorted critters, including Pepe le Pew, protect the holy space to the rear. However, it is Bagpuss who reigns supreme in his fetching, pink stripe pyjamas. Leading from the front, that "old fat furry Catpus" heralds in the oncoming, wondrous world of PJs and DJs and a marvellous, mechanical, mouse-owned pipe organ. Are they really here to mend me? Already "loose at the seams" where am I in Bagpuss's awakening dreams? Without him and his reveries, we and the other Yafflites are nothing. To him is given the Biggest Story, even bigger than Jackanory or what was hidden in the weekly hexagonal Music Box. Surprise is everywhere. I follow.

"Here is a box, a musical box, wound up and ready to play. But this box can hide a secret inside. Can you guess what is in it today?"

As my Heart Chest opens I find myself looking in at myself as just one of a million scrutinising eyes in the sky. Fascinated, but growing self-conscious, I chew on the borrowed gum of eucalyptus leaves. The dry cave world of my mouth that tastes like the tarmac of car-parks explodes with flavour whilst giving quick jaw relief. I have to keep dancing to maintain the correct level of activity and agitation to journey, but I need to blot out the distractions of the disco-Now. As I chew and inhale the vapours the kangaroo within me regains his bounce and social bearings. *Skippy* arrives, dusty and bushwhacked from another adventure, but ready to lead me on through my past. He hops ahead.

Fidgeting, the Saturday Fleapit Kids and I bundle into our cheap seats. We are all lost in weekly catch up of *Wacky Races,* some madder than the *Banana Splits* with their defunct Magic Machine and craziness. Hairs from the *Hair Bear Bunch* get everywhere, even now. The Potty Timers grin on playing historical games in saucepan tin helmets with puppets and invisible fleas that, quite sensibly, try to escape the circus of their strange circumstance.

A sudden tornado, issuing from the *Tasmanian Devil* at my feet, arrives on the dance floor to find me as small and meek as a town house Danger Mouse. I have become a quiet Vanishing Point in the far-flung Universe; a reluctant Superhero holding a bomb with a rapidly diminishing, fizzing lit fuse. I pass it on to the other members of The High Explosive gang who are all busy checking their watches by the old Town Hall clock that tells the time "steadily, sensibly; never too quickly, never too slowly" for all the Trumptonites still dancing.

Captain Flack does a quick roll call to check who is present: "Pugh! Pugh! Barney McGrew! Cuthbert! Dibble! Grubb!" The group confirms that they are all here, if not fully present, at least accountable as I continue to dance through the excitable night. It is a big crowd now as everyone collides in super group consciousness. It is adult playtime as even the precocious pigs Pinky and Perky are here in their bibs and braces, flouting their farmyard fads and fashion.

A group of passing wayward girls from St. Trinian's up hockey sticks and beat the best of Grange Hill whilst smoking, gambling, swigging moonshine and out horsing the law. In the cascading feathers from their exploding pillows we all act out the Midnight Kid, would-be Naughty Boys and bad schoolboys frolicking one and all, when Rupert, Rollo and Raggety arrive from Nutwood to sort us out. They pull up our working class socks into the sprightly, more organised, adventures of the middle classes.

The impeccably dressed Bear with chequered scarf and matching trousers finds so many friends. He is not lost unlike those bears initially left at stations. Poor Paddington – how he tugs on all our hearts! These days, the overcrowded trains are full of struggling Twenty-First century Witches and Wizards looking for the invisible, divisible platform at King's Cross, whilst my Dancing Bear and I are left looking for midnight, marmalade sandwiches in the secret compartments of suitcases from darkest Peru.

...We'd give you a part, my love, but you'd have to play the fool. Wow! wow! wow! wow! wow! unbelievable!...

It is *'Wow'* now as we enter the portals of Supermarionation Land. Brains, Penelope and Parker, like Pinocchio before them, all cut their strings and some slack to be here; so too the Captains Scarlet and Black, handsome and brooding as ever. The angels Melody, Harmony and Symphony dart by on heavenly, sky sent missions of war to bring earthly peace. Joe 90 is all of a go-go as the Thunderous Birds take off to save humanity from disasters at the puppet event horizon. Like them, I am dancing outside my skin as my free-spirited soul races through electric, cosmic-coloured strings.

...You better watch out you better beware...Albert said that E equals M C squared...

On the outer edges of the ever-growing frontiers of the physical Universe, dancing resembles being on board the *Starship Enterprise* riding the thought waves of Einstein's expanding intellect under the mind-expanding tutelage of Buddha. As a pioneering space-explorer I enter Dark Space and bump into the enemies of the galactic Who Doctor. They still frighten both those hidden behind the safe, sheltering backs of sofas and those dancing deliriously on the dance floor. Is it me so afraid, yet free flying?

Flipping in and out of time, overseeing the saving and destroying of worlds, the Doctor becomes consumed like us by the annihilating threat of Daleks,

Steel Men, Yetis and sinister Masters. Fu Manchu is in me and you; evil genius enough to ruin us all. Nearby some Mysterons scuttle in the dark shadows spreading their fear. I call upon Spectrum and tap into my healing powers of 'retro-metabolism' to complete my night mission.

For a moment I am scared. Friday-fright Hammer Horror sends me the Black Magic shivers, but I swerve just in time to avoid the Void and catch myself from falling into the outer reaches of the Night Mind and the Dawning Diabolical. I turn away from a Dark Door – an opportunity missed, but a lighter event horizon emerges as a result. Not for me a path of darkness as the spiralling Tunnel-of-Time turns back from black to funnelling white. I dip to the right and encounter Moon Base Alpha, to the left is unchartered territory and spinning, unfriendly UFOs.

In my current state I need to keep myself positive. Luckily, *Casey Jones* tugs on his whistle and wakes me up. He beckons to me – all aboard the fast train back to the Galactic Dynamic. Where is my ticket? He gives me a wink and a free ride. As I board my meditational focus suddenly slips and I am left wondering if I am that man …*leaving, on that midnight train to Georgia…goin' back to a simpler place and time…?* Lost in my dancing I have no idea where I am. I simply have to trust.

Steaming through the rising musical sentiment is *H R Pufnstuf*. He is going be my friend when things get rough. Like Jesus. No *Witchiepoos* here, simply the awe-inspiring wonder of kid's TV and the believable magic of old tape reels. Finally, in front of me, rising from the centre of a tranquil lake, a gushing fountain of purity springs – the backdrop to the Champions Swiss HQ or the true source of all ESP?

The telepathic density of the Veil thins and in my altered state access to the Spectral Light of All is now possible as the last of the encroaching Shadows finally retreat. I tune out the Nightmare channel and my consciousness heads back toward the dance floor and my special Homeland Heroes. On my return to my body I find I am all right. I have escaped to the safety of Witch Mountain, but 'Sssh!', tell no one. It has been a Secret Squirrel affair.

…You should be dancing, yeah…dancing, yeah…

Immediately back on the dance floor a retro-musical-medley takes my boogying thoughts and gesturing arms elsewhere. In the limited space I begin to finger disco, performing old familiar patterns. *Saturday Night Fever* lights the fuse and starts the spark, reminding me of all the teenage dance routines hastily fashioned and rehearsed in bedrooms to new Top 40 Tunes taped weekly from the radio. Sunday practice becomes religious.

Grease continued the hits, the lines and hips *...you're the one that I want, oh, oh, oh...* as I wiggled through the fuzz and acne-filled months of the youthful years. Dance replaced the need for sex and dating, and for a while defended me from my sexuality as the romantic, sugar-haze God of the Great Big Malt Shop in the Sky beamed down and beckoned. Entwining with the fabulous teenage moves and grooves is the legendary Boogaloo refrain as we danced ourselves D-d-d-d-d-d-d-d-dizzy. Now we do it once more.

...Dance, dance, dance, tonight, we'll leave the world behind...this is dynamite...tonight...

Turning like Tibetan children on prayer wheels we hold hands and lean back, swinging under the glitter ball until we all fall about laughing, feeling wonderfully sick. Likewise, how we had so much fun spinning *Off the Wall* all those years ago as so many drunken funky monkeys. Then the amazing tunes, visitations and atmospherics enter in as ABBA arrives. Some things get serious. They were so good, so important. *...No desire to run...neither you nor I'm to blame when all is said and done...* I listen and learn in order to survive a divorcing world.

Elvis Presley, Barbara Streisand, Bette Midler, The Carpenters, Dolly Parton, Joni Mitchell, John Denver, Glen Campbell, The Who, The Jam, Elton

John, The Sex Pistols, The Stranglers, Diana Ross, The Bee Gees, and Donna Summer are just some of the fantastical bedfellows writhing and entwining in strange teenage sheets. As fanatical followers and members of appreciation societies we all dress up and copy. Tom Jones and Shirley Bassey out-sing them, whilst the mercurial Queen Freddie entertains and gets into bed with them all. Genesis happens. The Police arrive.

...Roxanne, you don't need to put on the red light...those days are over...you don't need to sell your body to the night...

More doors open as in walk the Banshee and Punk heroes who captured my Indie mind and imagination. Spoon-feeding my soul with their melodies, words and strange songs, the psychedelic conceits and presence of Pink Floyd, Siouxsie Sioux, and David Bowie jangle in the tangled dream-weave.

...John, I'm only Dancing...

Bowie is a Jene Genie all right, posing as Jean Genet in night disguise. Everything becomes about Inspiration, Sound and Vision. Kate Bush arrives. Her muse thrills, filling the psyche and surrounds the house and bedroom walls with mysticism, pop and poster art. In her dreamtime, handfuls of spirit and reality are psychologically shared. Her musical warrior perks up our ears as she sends her Shiva, music-tipped arrows hurtling through the air straight to the mind and heart.

Later on, The Smiths join in with their sing-a-long-a-suicide cheery guitar riffs and clever poetry *...the leather runs smooth on the passenger seat...* They remind us to *Hang the DJ* or at least down thumbs and boo them if they are not playing the rhythms and tunes of our life. As modern-day Celebrants spreading the love, we follow happy tunes, not miserable music. Those of us who dance and bop must be allowed to do so freely without too much interruption to individual artistry by DJs spinning their indulgent egos and over-extending introductions.

...I'll go where your music takes me...where your rhythm makes me...that's where my destiny is gonna be...

Sound should lift up not grind down and jagged transitions are anathema to the night-journeying, dawn-driven disco soul. The war of musical evolution for those of us 'dancing our light' in Club Land continues when some fantastic, high-kicking Cossacks arrive. They surround me and take me away from my grumbling, prosaic thoughts. I am wonderfully surprised as they open up the gypsy highways to the fast-flying skies.

…And the people that you meet wanna open you up like Christmas…I'm a classy honey, kissy huggy, lovey dovey ghetto princess…

Some nu-disco and electroclash mixes with the usual pop and glam rock. The airways are filled with elevating music. All for the joy of the Melodious Angels in my expanding wings and the Rhythmic Devils in my feet I dare to dance to a different beat. So much swaying, and so many soft shoe shuffles and recollections, are connected to musical memories and the young, formative, inner creation of the transforming self.

In a free-fall of reminiscences I relive and remember them so I can shake them off and re-grow in the now. Then a re-mixed, slow interweaving riff gives a gentler lift whilst reminding of us the need to take stock …*Do you know where you're going to? Do you like the things that life is showing you?*… Oh yes, oh yes I do! Well, in this current moment, but life has not always been like this.

So I spiral within myself, instinctively following the inner wave as it curls inspirationally. Gliding without a surfboard I do not know whether I am going up or down so I vortex around and round until I remember that …*Every one of us has a Heaven inside*… Agility and courage are needed to get there, as well as the more useful thieving and shepherding skills, yet still I need to dance in order to remember as well as forget. Surrounded by influential memories I know that it is imperative that they are all offered up into the Sacred Flame. I tip my cup, empty my overstuffed cupboards, and check in my ignorance as I grab myself a fistful of instant gratification. Who knows what will remain?

Running through my dancing body and Mind's Eye, emotional expression and theatre waxes as the Moon climbs over the wall to whispered words in a *Cruel Garden*. Now, it is a hand-clapping, thigh-slapping, foot-stomping *Blood Wedding* as art and technical discipline takes over from early teenage fun. The magic of a slow mimed scene from the flowering imagination of Kemp enchants, whilst the sculptural androgynous form and boyish charm of Michael Clark, with his exquisite lines, curving shoulders and beautiful feet, make him an edible punk angel. He would have made a wonderful faun *midi*.

...Express yourself, don't repress yourself...

Astaire and Kelly arrive and air-glide by, keeping things effortlessly smooth and strong. In fluid extension Baryshnikov dances along. My medallion man Travolta struts by. MJ spins in. Heady student Laban days turn into theatrically captivating Bausch nights. Stomping on, The Cholmondeleys vanguard their contemporary presence. AMP blossoms into electric adventures. DV8 agitate and excite.

Meanwhile, the Looney Tunes of my own La-La and Never Land gather at the Pearly Gates ahead. I perceive the twin Pillars of Hercules looming, inviting, as the Guitar Wizard and Pinball King greet me on either side. Behind them assemble a crowd of friendly Faces, Visitors and some unexpected Saints. *…I'm not denying, we're flyin' above it all…hold my hand, don't let me fall…oh show me Heaven please…* I can feel the Rapture only a bump and a grind away.

So I enter into the House of Spirit whilst simply swaying away to a good disco tune on the living breath of inspiration. At last the host, the Holy Ghost – she is here.

"Still dancing?" I hear someone ask from a gathering spiritual crowd.

"Yes," I reply, not knowing who on earth is speaking, but smiling at them anyway. "I love dancing."

"We know," chorus the ghostly Passing Visitors. "We've been watching."

They explain that is why I placed music in the soles of my feet before I was born. It is true. One way or another I enjoy dancing more than anything else, and tonight I do so once more in the Rediscovery of Disco. Gloriously orchestrated tonal tunes and anthems capture my heart and feet. It is an inherent chaos of popular melodies and delight to be steadily worked through. I am Old School, you see, where the Golden Oldies still sooth the soul and delight, whilst the Indies give the mind some bite.

In this moment of pleasure, prioritising dance, music and song, I become spellbound as an invisible hand takes hold of me in a rhythmic swirl. Turned in this manner I become partnered by the Improvisational Spirit of the other side and affirm loudly that …*Oh yes Sir, I can boogie, but I need a certain song…I can boogie, boogie woogie, all night long…* I do not worry about hesitation or reputation, but am unsure if I will leave anyone begging for more!

"How are you doing?" the Visitors ask, genuinely concerned. They know I have been struggling with the clash and conflict of recent events.

"I'm doing fine," I lie cheerfully, as you would to your parents to cover up the mess you call life and use as an excuse for personal style. "All over the place, but fine."

The Visitors laugh. Enquiring, I wonder if it gets any better than this, but they just laugh again. They know I am presently more than a tiny bit bothered, a little bewitched and a whole lot bewildered. The higher echelons of the Spirit World are beautifully light, piercingly bright, and rather mind numbing as their frequencies scramble my everyday brain. It is hard to find the words to express the states that they provoke. How can you capture a moment of Golden Silence? How do you find words for wordless richness?

At this point I wish I could paint and splash my story through spinning colour. Behind, and off to one side, the Spirit Room filled with writers is encouraging, but less than impressed with my inarticulacy. I can hear all their Stage Lefts, Blimey O'Reilly's and Bugger Me's. Without physical bodies they are not always sympathetic to the corporeal condition and push me on to breakthrough. For them I am just a job.

"No," I inform them, "I can't go any faster." Yet I wish I could for my plodding slowness often frustrates me.

My Grandmother intervenes and concurs. She tells me not to rush, but to get on with it and suggests in future a speed-typing course might be beneficial. The spool of my mind's typewriting ribbon has become unravelled. The reality is that I have got myself into a muddle and like a ball of wool I need help to be unpicked. Tight-knotted strands of light running up and down my spine and around my head must be combed free. It requires the practiced skilful fingers of spiritual leaders, the patience of Saints and the support of good friends.

…See baby we've been too strong for too long…

I need to stop and sort myself out, but I am too dizzy, too exhilarated and exhausted, to do it by myself. The Overshadowing Host, she that is goodness, perceives the need of my weave and sends her servants, the scuttling spiders, to help me realign. In her quick, spinning fingers and their silk-dispersing spinnerets everything is possible. A wonder web is spun about me and chakras fly open as I commune with Things Higher.

Alongside dancing, connecting to gods, angels and spirits has always been a part of my life, Nature and the True Way of things. Sometimes it has been so strange, so difficult, but always they have sought to bring me solace and upliftment. *…Many battles must he win 'till he earns his place on earth like the other creatures do…* Did I battle enough when Times got tough? *…Will there be a happy end now that all depends on you…* All I know is that I must not give up, not now, not ever.

…Supernature, supernature, supernature, supernature…

So I scratch out a survivor's post-Christmas, dance floor surface living by talking turkey to the invisible crowd amassing over my shoulder – friends, family members (known and unknown), and all the Prophets of the Wild: Holy Moses, M'Lady, Mary, Saint John and the Smokin' B'Jesus. It is a maverick pack, all right, but I love them all and have so much to be thankful for in their help, guidance and on-going, over-seeing presence.

...We're lost in music, caught in a trap, no turning back...feel so alive, I quit my 9 to 5...we're lost in music...

Reeling in the music I find dancing helps me like that. It is a good place to be, the best place for me, particularly in the recent grim wring of the Dishcloth of Life. Pain has hit us as hard as pain can be and trouble comes in battalions so we can earn our spurs. Cancer has taken one, but not the other, and we have lost a few others recently along The Way – three friends and three family members within the last year and a half. Like an adult I tried to hold it all together, but like a child I secretly sobbed into my pillow at night until the tears ended, the pain dissolved, and Life began to dance again, despite myself.

...It's lonely out in space...on such a timeless flight...

Motion carries us on to smarter evolutionary moves; e-motion the energy behind the muscular grooves. Flowing in the face of adversity, the love of love, and hopefully your job, keeps you moving. Life is short and is becoming shorter. Now, back in the saddle, I am dancing again; an overdue return to the real me, whoever that is and might turn out to be!

Yet the Illusions of Life are strong including the art of all of this, which keeps me caught and bound. Let it not be so. A Water Bearer arrives and we juggle bottles, beers and chewing gum. The latter becomes an offering between adjacent tribes as the ever-growing concentric circles of dance, fun and friendship spread and engulf those stomping nearby. Social dance seems to remain mainly an individual activity these days although we like dancing in twos, threes and fours. Old popular Pavanes and galloping Gavottes, reels and gigues, Latin and Ballroom, are frowned upon on the modern club dance floor, yet I wonder if Quentin Crisp would have approved of such blokes and belles in ball gown style?

I turn to see that the recently widowed has now joined us still dealing with deep grief, intensity and suicidal despair. Occasional laughter through a falling face and a veil of tears, his tragedy releases and we pray that he will pull through in his recent god-awful, sad circumstance. Womb-like, his aura empties in an attempt to start again, but he cannot let go, cannot integrate the essentials and essences of his great love, not just yet. In some ways he never will for Life has changed suddenly, irrevocably. *...Miles and miles of empty space inbetween us...* We walk a few steps in his shoes on his solitary journey. He feels like a fledgling that must leave the nest and start again; so like the trembling calf he once birthed, trying to stand and walk for the very first time.

Around us dance the many survivors who are left behind still connected in love with men buried in the past who have now become their guardian angels. We help and talk as we stand by on International Rescue whilst looking out upon the Sea of Shifting Scenes being enacted before us. There are so many fascinating roles for us and our fellow brothers and sisters to play through. In the attachment and detachment of parts given to us in this world of human activity, compassion is all we can ask for to help us through. In our duration of the life-death arc that is our given span – one hand long in the millions of lives that are ours, a mere coffee spoon to others and those souls overseeing – Love is the ever accompanying madness and mystery.

The angels take their fair share of our spuming 'grace' energy for better use elsewhere, but they support us in our efforts too. I turn to the Professor for advice, but he reminds me that he is, first and foremost, just a blonde. Before emeritus and beyond eminence, his taciturnity means that my basic question on elements and chemistry sets must wait. Momentarily silenced, I turn back to the magic beat of my rhythmic feet, but my questing mind soon begins to turn over. ...*Keep on with the Force, don't stop...don't stop 'til you get enough...*

I somehow still believe the answer lies in the metaphysics of the astrolabe, and I know that the maths and sciences underlying the human equations are bubbling away underneath whether I understand their alchemical connection or not. The processes of Realisation are like cooking. It is all in the preparation, mixing and baking – the ingredients are there, it only requires the right temperature and the correct amount of Time and Love.

...*MacArthur Park's is melting in the dark...and I'll never have that recipe again...oh no...*

I wonder what kind of cake I would make. After all, Love is purely the passion of adding and eating; a living covenant to explore not a man-made contract to merely uphold. All thoughts of baking and philosophy are suddenly lost in the distant drone of a megaphone and excited bouncing. ...*Video killed the radio star...video killed the radio star...in my mind and in my car, we can't rewind we've gone too far...* Innocent musical mind games go on.

Whilst I usually like biting on apples and pondering on the imponderables, all juicy food for thought, Schrödinger's cat will have to wait. In my recent decoherence I do not worry too much about whether I have put the milk out and the cat in the fridge by mistake. It will all sort itself out in the end. There is too much space between particles to do anything but be happy as the world constantly arranges and re-arranges itself around us in its intricate magnetic forming and colourful patterning.

I move on to dance with Sue, he of the Cobbling Shoes and Quick Fingers. He is perspicacious and a lover of responsibility, bamboo shots and shoestrings. As a father of two girls, he is used to dealing with the many ways of messing with minds. He is an intelligent panda, so we speak of allegiance to dragons from around the world and the evolutionary war of languages. Strictly Un-Ballroom, we forsake discipline in favour of a loose Latin style, merengue and salsa, as we boldly take the law into our own fun hands whilst enjoying the re-socialising. We manage to tie ourselves up in semi-choreographed knots of cobbled together social dance, half remembered and mostly fumbled.

...Let's stick together, c'mon, c'mon let's stick together...

The invading far away words ring true. We have all taken vows of some sort or the other as we explore the social avenues of love, friendship and commitment, but fidelity and loyalty remain divided matters. Some cheat secretly. In these situations Sue usually chooses to remain firmly in adulthood, so averts his eyes and tries not to look at the frolicking nonsense and reprehensible behaviour of some of those around. There is too much on his own plate to attend to, but he understands the sense and sensibility and need for dancing and a rollicking good night out.

Unsolicited, yet wisely, Three passing Monkeys – See No, Hear No, and Speak No – try to explain and advise us, but there are no evils to be found here. A fourth Mischievous Monkey crosses his arms and shuts his mouth in a sensible bid to do no harm, but a fifth closeted Flying Angry Monkey, unemployed since the downfall of the Wicked Witch of the West, attacks and annoys us without charm. Sue and I turn away pretending we do not care …*If it don't fit don't force it, let it happen naturally*… and continue to dance regardless of hostile stares and groundless insinuations of rudeness. Yet somehow umbrage is unnecessarily taken.

After some minutes of couple dancing, serious prestidigitation, and neurological knitting and dexterity of the highly coordinated kind, I turn to find the secure naval one, Sooty, aka the Ginger Dream Genie. He has regressed to childhood madness and cuckoos around the place, happy as the Lamb Larry and the High Fives. He is such a great mate, a first class passenger awaiting departure in the Lunatics Lounge. Their trio friend Sweep stands by, a barefoot native warrior, a cool Dudey in search of love-sex and the right International Man. German, Spanish or an American? ...*Sky rockets in flight, afternoon delight*... All are still on the potential menu.

"Love is the Wisdom; Freedom the Heavens," whispers a nearby passing soul of a Saint in a Sweet Jesus reverie.

Somehow, I need to get by him and his irksome manner. Two prisons deep, that particular Saint found out the Soft Light in the dark in a very hard way, but it does not need to be like that. Humility can lead you there instead, that and becoming like a child, or in his case the letting go of misogyny and the letting in of Mother God. Whilst he is preoccupied by the satisfaction of spouting his own wisdom I steal a large set of keys from his belt. The Universe instantly informs and warns me that there are an awful lot of doors to explore so I best choose well. Moments of magic like these appear and disappear so quickly.

So, ever on and always up, I double bow the ribbons on my dancing shoes to ensure safety and strive for disco gold again. Home and warmth are upper most in the evolutionary scale which is why I must go to God through the hearth of my heart, dancing in the flower flames of rising fire and happy in the principle of sharing. There are so many good people to meet in Life, so much still to learn from each other at the Old Earth School of Knocks of Consciousness, including that one 'Pythonesque Monty' who is deliberately, exquisitely not. It turns out that "We're all individuals" after all.

Grit, grazes and more Lessons in Love than we can shake a stick at are to be found here on Gaia's multifaceted surface. Over my shoulder, a dear many-year-dead friend of mine grins and shouts a sweet refrain, a reminder to keep positive...

"Don't let the bastards wear you down," he says, grinning.

It is Alfie. I still remember fondly the afternoon we spent having tea with the ghosts. He did not like it then, a bit too Spooksville for his liking, but in their revealing presence they were real and true, constant companions from beyond our everyday reckoning. I came with a Haunting, but they would not leave him alone even after I had left and was long gone. He knew that they had come to take him. Being an Angel of Death, of helping those to pass and cross, is not always easy, but such honour comes with brave weeping and the lifting up of the veil.

"Thanks Alfie," I reply silently, smiling, but not really convinced. "Thanks a lot."

Alfie nods and points to a floating Elysian field passing by. I start to run and dance through the Heavens towards the Fortunate Isles of the Blessed. Bemused, I seek out inspiration in strange places, but all is not as it seems. Past memories and mysteries of fairy woods, jungles and the odd ways of men flash by. Ethereal Feys and Will-O-The-Wisps drift by enthralling, whilst some Hairy Dwarves and Wood Gnomes gather around to stare up at me.

In a flash, short and tall free spirits take over including some Flibbety-Gibbets and their Fly-By-Night bedfellows. Faintly Macabre fascinates whilst the Dyads and Triads, Monads and Dryads, entrance in odd floating patterns and floral partnerships. The Elves are here plucking their lyres and singing. Am I lost in the Land of Fairies? Entranced, not looking where I am going, I stumble into a nest of Rumbling Pixies who dangerously nibble at my ankles and push me off my current cloud of Partial Paradise. Alfie laughs.

"That'll teach you," he says before disapparating and leaving me alone.

There is only one way to tumble, sulkily with a small 'hmph!', but I try to enjoy the descent however disgruntled. My first attempt at flight fails, but I am on my toes ready to pick myself up again, endlessly so it seems. If that way did not work I will simply have to experiment and concoct another. Meanwhile, the earthier grounding elements bring me back to the dance and social swing of the Hustler Happening.

The Passage of Time is suddenly with us. Where have the years flown to and why do I feel so youthful? Have I really failed to grow up or does everyone still feel young on the inside? Are we all eternally light whilst experiencing the different seasons of life and ourselves in the passing of years? The splashing Fountain of Universal Love energises all things bright and beautiful, all things great and small. My spirit is willing; is my mortal flesh so weak? Is regeneration possible to those parts of us that ail, fail and fall? Back to the Ball.

Next to me Captain Chaos practises precarious balancing and flying positions with outstretched arms. Whee! Look how he goes. ....*And you know how it feels to reach too high, too far, too soon...you saw the whole of the moon...* I love the Captain and see the flying me in him. Trusting the whim I copy and follow and we are suddenly in simultaneous take-off. As we fly sky-high on our lunar mission we bump into the boy called Buttons struggling with his little bit of innocent bi-curiosity. We circle the ceiling together.

Around us, hanging from the walls and rafters, cascading from on top of podiums, I notice the Hibiscus People flower, all pink and peach, thriving on the rising equatorial heat. ...*Lookin' for some hot stuff baby this evenin'...* Nimrod helps himself to their nectar as a Rose of Jericho blows through – a survival, revival, desert souvenir of the Sacred Heart of You. I glide through the verdant emerald green of their disco scene, pushing through the bushes and branches bearing low-hanging fruit to soar above the top of their tall transforming trees.

It is easy to get lost in the telepathic Kingdom of Plants. The Baby Bios and new plant food generation bloom, but I must beware the troubling Triffids that lurk and loom in between. ...*Burn baby burn! – burn that Mama down...* In the Hothouse of Potentiality, exotics and tropics grow everywhere. Some Inadvertent Furtives creep around the sides of the dance floor showing off, whilst trying to look shy. Others dance and sway, naturally burgeoning. Ancient ferns of the forest unfurl. Branches of blossom come into bud and bloom. There is flora and fauna everywhere.

As people warm up the night gets hotter. It is becoming a *Disco Inferno* all right so we take off our shirts – some need help in this now seemingly complex task – revealing faded-tanned stomachs and pink plimsoll lines. Going native, we are inhabitants of a semi-naked world as other disrobing bears gather around. Shared energy pulses between us as our feet gather speed and the momentum steadily builds. A different door opens and a further opportunity for lift-off is presented. I take my chances and run a million miles without leaving the spot. ...*Be running up that road, be running up that hill, with no problems*... I need to muster my fire energy. Beneath my dancing feet sparks ignite; combustion is all as I break free from any remaining chains.

On hot coals I speed through the World of Flames, their tongues licking at my feet like a tango, a fantastic fandango, into the arms of a Rascally Devil. ...*It was the heat of the moment telling me what my heart meant*... Dancing for liberty, for freedom and for the sheer joy of it, my body surfs for expression caught in a brief musical moment. Suddenly alive, I become 'spontaneous-dance.com'. This is who I am right now and who the future me encourages and beckons me on to be. Watery feelings and fire meet. ...*Steamy windows*... Sweltering, the lenses of perception are cleansed and I am on the verge of breaking free into the over-spin of the One Bright Light.

...*Ch-ch-changes...just gonna have to be a different man...time might change me, but I can't trace time*...

Now even the changes are changing and nothing is the same anymore, especially not any of this. Caught in the living process between products of Am and Be, words and thoughts only add to the mental illusion. I need to be free from them in pure exhilaration. In search of the non-fading True Reality I dance upon a newfound path of Awareness and perceive that which has ever been and is Unchanging. ...*This state of independence will be*... It was waiting for me alongside the many different aspects of Universal Joy that I try to capture in exaltation of angels. The passing Wingèd Ones and I have one thing in common – we all seek the Golden Flame housed in the Temple of Heaven.

...*Freedom come, Freedom go...Freedom want, Freedom stay...Freedom love then she flies away...Freedom never stay long...Freedom moving along...*

Transmutation is on my mind now, as the fires of consciousness rise and burn the residue of unwanted, un-useful, stuck thoughts and feelings of deep me. Here come the life-affirming colours, the reds, oranges and yellows, like flames flickering and surging through the blood's warm maroon. Vibrations pulse through my body as integrating elements of sound, breath and movement. Music and dance heal as they break down the old, harmonise the new, and help me move on. ...*I'm picking up good vibrations*... Their forces baffle and amuse as law and order are lost and confused in the higher fight for comedy right and chaos magic. Buster Keaton and Charles Chaplin run amok as my many sub-personalities rise to the fore. The past comes back to haunt.

Suddenly it is mayhem as clogging folk, country dancers and Whirling Dervishes swirl by in the whisking disco mists, yet all must be offered up in the fiery re-gathering. The spectres of old ghostly halls and gate-crashed balls, of courtly dance, of meetings and greetings, of grief and happiness throughout the many centuries, all converge here. The catalysts and converters hidden within re-interpret the swirling recollections of social memory and those reminiscences of distant trodden boards like a filmic experience.

Somehow separated from my body, I look down at the gang and my jigging self from the ceiling like a bemused chameleon suspended in mid-air, clutching the chain of glitter ball, alert, yet silent. I find I am turning silver in my attempt to blend in. Lasers and lights hit. Blinding, everything becomes mirrored and mosaic. My mind bends. In the rainbow cascade I fall. How can I encompass this all? Rapidly returning to my body on the dance floor I find I am back in the crowd, just one more laughing lost adrift in the musical mingle. Yet a new toe-tapping identity beckons so I mix it all up and give it back out in acts of daring and difference.

Yet how, and why on Earth now, and with you, this group, my beloved and I? Ten leaping lords, a dancing bear and a somnambulist chameleon caught sleep-dance awakening. ...*Wake me up before you go-go...* Rip Van Winkle comes down from the mountain at last. Yet wading through the spiritual altitudes and forming mists of confusion it is like a game of No Cluedo. Am I smart enough to be my own super sleuth and hunt my Ever-Self down? A fusion conclusion methinks.

Yet any old furrowed fights and fears of mine are soon subdued, ironed out and lost to the beat of the best disco in town – extra, extra large and attitude free. A passing group of disobedient and disbelieving angels all wave at me. Peering at them I am unsure as to which side of the Veil I inhabit. ...*Through the flame and the fury...will tomorrow survive when two worlds collide...* When realms converge edges seemingly blur. However, the Universe insists on sharpening the blunt Sword-of-my-Mind on the hard Edge-of-its-Truth in order to go the distance for the work ahead. Dancing comes easy, clear thinking and words do not. Yet there ...*Ain't no stopping us now...we're on the move...* and I am in the blessed groove.

An unwitting angel stands behind me, holding me in his arms. He defibrillates my heart with his tapping fingers 344 times in one song. Speaking in ET finger code some passing aliens bubble under in their glittery disco space suits. Will they be good to us and take us to our intergalactic home? Everyone has one, it is just a matter of remembering and asking the way.

...Arcadia x-ray x-ray delta niner niner zero...this is Starfleet control...you are clear to go hyper space... acknowledge...

Stupidly I look for trans-light in every passing starship trooper, when I know it is hidden deep within me *...Affirmative, Star-com we have situation gold...* but still they take my breath away. I call out to the occupants of the passing *'...interplanetary, quite extra-ordinary...'* craft. They turn out to be inter-dimensional angels and galactic space captains. Have I left Planet Earth and reached Sky City?

In the thinning atmosphere my Thumping Heart tunes into the rising disco rhythms and my pulses rise by the beat per minute. The Archangels Gabriel and Michael gang up and do me the honour of uniting in the Heavens slipstream above as their rays of light focus on my crown. A third strand of silvery stars entwine as Raphael joins in with the Laurels and Hardys. I am told that Uriel cannot be with us today as he is busy preparing work for an upcoming sun project. It is a shame that he has to miss out, but I am sure he will get to make it up somehow.

...I will be the one who loves you until the end of time...

Suddenly suspended in space, an unexpected, yet beauteous drop of grace descends, amber, green and sparkling gold. For a moment I feel like a ripening grape receiving the dawn rays through the dissolving early morning mist, plumpening in a simple life of loveliness. It is all that I desire and so much more than me. Love is the drug and bead of blood necessary for real people dealing in fairness and honesty of transaction in the shopping of Humanity and Honey Bees.

...It's that little souvenir of a terrible year, which makes me wonder why...

Overseen by the Other Side, I suddenly belong to multiple schools of thought, flitting and cross-pollinating ideas. The passing Angels and Advisors of the Other Side synthesise and sooth our souls with their creamy dollops scooped from the jar of the Balm of Gilead that they hold. Lotus leaves unfurl. Rose petals break from their bunched flowers spreading their pungent beauty. Goodness surrounds us all around. The Lily falls as the Witching Hour arrives and takes hold of us. The deep roots of music sway the body and sweeps clean the corners of my mind.

...In the midnight hour I will wait for you, wait for you, I will wait for you...

Altered states become tribal now; the fire-child Cinderella is at the Ball after all. Demented by sudden freedom and extreme restriction, she dances until she drops at the Moan of Midnight and runs across the courtyard. As she exits, a secret crystalline slipper falls upon a step. A reminder of what has been, what has left and what might still come to pass. The Weirds and Eeries enter in stage right with a fright and a flap of their bat like wings. Behind them Jacob Marley is here with his unfortunate ghostly wutherings, newfound love and bejewelled cushions. Christmas eve has already passed and we are all the better for it. Another glorious notch carved into the trunk of the Tree of Life.

Dramatically, a Dark Knight swoops in to cut a swathe between us. He moves one step forward, two steps to the side, battling bishops with an eye on the Fair, but fed up, Queen. I ask if the King is in, but I am told that the security forces of the Stern Superiors, who are not so fond of the Beloved-Sisters-of-Perpetual-Over-Indulgence, have already carried out Willy Wonka. So that was who I saw being removed earlier. The group swarms to protect the Beleaguered

One, ousting the dark stranger and re-establishing social boundaries. We need no lancing hornets here.

...I'll forgive and forget if you say you'll never go...'cos it's true what they say...it's better the devil you know...

The prancing, dancing Jester and Fool is a wise and very merry soul indeed. His wisdoms make him one of my chosen advisory three for he has wept and laughed, laid to death many a friend and partner, yet re-found. He is the Music Maker of Weddings and Parties – the 70's Disco King. His ringing, singing sidekick angel revs up for revels and heads toward the bar. They will spend the rest of the night chasing each other in near-miss circles, collisions and crashes. Used to their farcical antics, we shall endure and love it all.

On the prospect of spotting more trouble than I can bear my bladder fortunately sends me signals that override my brain. I take a bathroom break and re-group in the men's washroom where I am overcome by a fiery wood sprite and an earthy hobgoblin. For unusual and specific, yet very different, reasons they make me laugh. Samantha gives me a free spray of her special scent – Heaven-Sent – and waves me away. She knows I can handle it whereas her hands are currently full of the wobbly-ones.

A strangely shaped, super-charged Cyclone-Wizard dries my fingers in an impressive flash.

Prodigiously zapped, I look at myself through a water-splashed mirror and smoothen what little, but unruly, hair I have. I notice that behind me a White-Rabbit runs down a wormhole in reverse. I trust his tunnelling instinct and follow him, coming up in another place in my mind as I bunny-hop back to the flock.

...I'm a different person, yeah...turn my world around...

On my return to the dance floor the undulating waves of Seasons and Cycles, of the murmuration and migration of flocks and shoals, all join in. Joy is steadily rising. The Sonics and Sonars sound as swallow, bat and turtle technology take over in a hypnotic flow of energy. The visuals cascade inside and out as I am enveloped and cocooned in colour. Auras fill and the emergent Butterfly Boy within readies to unfold his wings once more. The magnetic poles oppose, yet somehow hold; synthesis is the only useful answer.

...If I could read your mind, love, what a tale your thoughts could tell, just like a paperback novel, the kind the drugstores sell...

Above us all, in the Cosmic Sea of Souls, the Fisher of Man casts his mystic nets in a soul trawl. In the discombobulating Lagoon of Love people swim in, swarm, and swim back out again. Those on the fringes have more space to dance, but the Heart always wants to be in the centre of the huddle so that is where we find ourselves, but you have to be brave to dart between the jagged edges of the coral reef to get there.

Elbows and arms become fluid fins in the swimming as the splashing magic of music and dance takes over. The Dashing, the Daring and even the Down Rights all strut and stride, surfing toward mating, dating and the making of love, even if only for the hour or night. ...*Com'on make a move on me...* In the early hours it becomes time for more personal exotic displays from lips, hips and stroking fingertips.

...Oh you gotta feel me, heal me, chase me chase me...

The Vaseline Kids and the Slide and Glides are quickly in with their wonderful switchback moves. The serious dance-sexy crowd can easily take over wanting to make love to the quarter beats with their pounding, but unsensual love. Fortunately, my inner Nautch Indian dancing girl is strong and in control, so a bone-breaking session with any one of them is not on the cards tonight.

The Up For It are up for a bit, but they can all go drill a hole elsewhere. The Frenzies rise. I must not give in or I will fall into their lustful flames of orgiastic desire. Oops! Oh dear, never mind. Some move back three spaces, some do not pass go, whilst some do not collect two hundred. Others seemingly take it all. *...Gimme, gimme, gimme, a man after midnight...* Anything to get *...through the darkness to the break of the day...* Anything.

Whilst I dance alone others escort one another in their rhythmic writhing, enjoying the deliberate slip and trip as they accidentally fall onto the floor of a place that is sometimes called Purgatory. Others call it fun, release and exploration of the body. It does not really matter, for given time Nature will balance it all and the gold-rush Dancehalls of Excess will lead to the Palatial Abode of Wisdom in the end. Everything is simply necessary expressive energy and divine delight. Urges move us on as we dance between the states of other people's Heaven and Hell. Yet who arose and who truly fell?

...Sometimes I feel nobody gives me no warning...find my head is always up in the clouds in a dreamworld...it's not easy...living on my own...

Slowly, the smelting of seemingly unmeltable personal matter and built-up remains dissolve in the alchemical brew. Karma breaks down with work, ownership and Natural Law into its combustible molecules – astrological elements that alter in the fierce furnace of the Inferno. My soul releases from my body. It is 'Mok'sha' all right as my whole self burns up in acts of flame and conscious moxibustion. The shackles of shame and guilt break as I dance and simply ...*Blame it on the boogie*....

Apples of desire and self-knowledge have previously been eaten. Pride falls along with other outmoded states judged as sins. There were no bitter pills to swallow, I did it all for love. ...*Oh a little bit more, just a little bit more...* All for love. Now I shed my constricting burdens by dancing to infectious rhythms of recklessness, snagging the tops of my proverbial stockings on the jukebox jive.

Here, on the dance floor, even the surrendering of the mind to the heart is possible given time and a catchy tune. I lose myself to the liquidity of Love like a lump of brown sugar held onto the top of hot coffee before being slipped into the cup. My mind softens as all the rough angles and sharp surfaces of self dissolve. I toss back my head, shake out my mane and let my receding hair down; the usual number two with a little bit of fluff on top a la Hergé's adventurous hero.

...Knock on every door, tell them Love is the answer...life is a gift from above, we're blessed with soul...

The non-rebellion of my original youth shouts out so I take the chance to act the riotous teenage self in search of middle-aged realisation. It is much more fun now living life like a Duracell bunny operating on super-endurance mode. Surrounding unhappy disco bunnies and flat, fat bears are a sorry sight for sore eyes as we explode like indoor fireworks around them.

…I ain't never gonna let you go - don't go!…

Final take-off requires forgiveness of others and myself so Love embraces our mess and brings about the necessary upsurge of unselfconscious happiness. At the end of the day does any of it really matter? Here I go… I dance furiously trying to leave Life's complications and limitations behind. Somehow caught between motion and stillness I am spun out in a final act of soul-body separation.

…You make me feel mighty real…

Look! Here comes my hugging Huckleberry friend to save me from the frenzy of it all. My consciousness returns to the ever-shifting social scene that surrounds me and I am safely back in the secure arms of my dancing bear. He soundly stamps out the Here and Now, leaning his body weight upon me whilst ever smiling. I know he wonders where I have been, not because he wants to go there, but because in some ways I have been absent during my cosmic meandering and he has missed me.

What on earth could be more important than him? No earthly reason, only Heaven and a sense of wings with sky-bound purpose, yet I am reminded that …*Heaven is a place on earth*…. Having slipped from his fingers in my dancing fury, he now takes firm grasp and I am grateful for the holding, but still I feel the need to slip stream. Alongside my chameleon, a part of me is Western-astrological cat, part Eastern dragon, part playful dolphin and I must be free to roam and rise up through the starry night sky – always upstream against the emanating forces back toward the Source.

Firmly back in the saddle on the dance floor I momentarily surrender to earthly delight and dance marsupial like, the beleaguered quiet on my back in koala cuddles, expressing their exhaustion, camaraderie, and recently earned perplexities. Hugging and being hugged, I always feel better with someone in my arms connecting with the warmth of human touch. On this side of life we are just apes with big brains and dextrous thumbs and fingers after all.

Being thus securely held, any remaining sense of existential loneliness or meaninglessness no longer alarms me. My quilt is for sharing, a picnic blanket, not sleeping alone, although it does not matter for the Loving Heart is the True Inner Home and the Source of All Comfort. We just need to remember. Even in the saddest of days, with utterly exhausted will, there was always a glimmer of a good God.

Many years ago my loving Grandmother saved me from myself and a rapid exit to the Other Side in my hour of darkness. Since then Voices and Visions have flowed from a Spiritual World, but how do I share the Longest Journey that each must make – the final Home Coming – of which this initial experience of 'Mok'sha' is only the beginning.

Now, however, my refreshed perception still pushes on past the corners of my ordinary mind into the wide, blue yonder. The friendly face of the Dalai Lama comes back to smile and laugh at me, an ordinary Dalai La. Some marauding Native Americans cloak me in feathers as I shuffle my feet on the ground. Together we gather wampum beads to thread and share. Yet what do all these ghostly guides and cosmic gatherers want?

Mysteriously, my arms multiply like Shiva as Nataraja, Lord of the Dance. Mudras as quick as thrown lightening are everywhere. Movement becomes magic again as I free my encaged arms and throw off the mantle of togetherness. This journey I need to make on my own. ...*Then I get night fever, night fever...we know how to do it...* Juju to deep earth means I am as one entranced. Spellbound, I watch trapped earth and water bound souls release. The Marchioness goes down. Air, fire and metal souls rise around me. The Admiral Duncan goes up. From the bombs of Brixton, Brick Lane and Soho the no-to-hate-crime charity 17-24-30 is born reminding us once more that we are all in this together.

In a nearby invisible vigil, an angel holds up a candlelit lantern that emits such light that I can see into the black and the white of both worlds. As a result, many faces of those that have bravely passed before us float by in the veiled dark. Smokey O stands by on the other side laughing, blowing smoke rings straight at me. Dead these two years, he watches on and knows the joke is on the surviving us.

A few floating combustibles seen as lights and orbs attach to our group. We are honoured by their presence in the passing Dream-Wake. Some of the dead Elsies take a bow wanting to be named: Greg and Ben exit stage left, pursuant by Bernard the Bear whilst Kenny still kicks his legs high. They each have a grinning message for my heart, but where is the Consolamentum in that? They point to a growing blaze indicating that I have to pass through.

...We didn't start the fire...it was always burning since the World's been turning...

Casino Joe, Colorado's dead younger brother, arrives in full body form looking hot in black, white and red. Stakes are high now as I gamble with my soul, but no need for Faustian deals. I jump on a passing Devil's back and get him to take me through the Inferno on his dirty work. ...*Burn baby, burn...* I do not bother wrestling with my demons. I just dance with them until they are tired and give up and I am left the last one standing. What else can I do?

As I dance through the scorching blaze of flame, I turn my attention back to those dancing around me. Through the haze I see that the German angels are in with their super fine architecture, lines and design. They are smiling and hugging, not so much talking; ever grateful loving after their fearful moment of collapsing hearts. The French drizzle us with their oil and sunlit, carefree ways of ease. The Spanish all join in for the friendly fun and flamenco fiesta of it, whilst the Puerto Ricans trill their thrills. Duende is everywhere.

...One night in Bangkok and the world's your oyster...the bars are temples but the pearls ain't free...

Nearby, the Scottish Crew are in for a few reels, handsome as houses, oak-smoked and mature; their Italian puppy bounds around all passion and physical theatre. Like Christ, he is torn, but I see in him the free playful me. We cavort and improvise whilst others roll their eyes in dismay. Laughter erupts from the nephews and other young pups as they pinch an inch on the hips of us old 'uns; the lean years remembered in the fat of the Forties Land. They have it all yet to come and then some, whereas my life has reputedly only just begun.

Whatever the cause of my personal wounding the effects are licked and burnt away by the rising flames at the exit from the rocky Disco Cave. At the top of the world I just need to push through the final vent. From the soles of my stamping feet to the clap of my hands I dance through the fire of it all. The grief, anger and passion of past hurts, the trials and tribulations of the World's Troubles, are all part of my Transfiguration as I near final breakthrough.

...Love is a burning thing, and it makes a fiery ring, bound by wild desire, I fell into a ring of fire...I went down, down, down and the flames went higher, and it burns, burns, burns...

Fags and Faggots go up in flame and smoke around me. There is nothing here to hold onto, nothing here to help in the gulping of combustible gases and thinning air. However enticing the vertiginous heights seem, one part of me staunchly tries to remain grounded, a simple *...Slave to the rhythm...* Descent? Ascent? Why are those mountainous peaks moving so rapidly towards me?

Who knew they could be so vast and beautiful. Is it I that they beckon to in a bid to come climb?

Some sprightly, old goats of Toledo appear, those Old Masters with ruffled white collars. They yodel and stroke their beards as they gather around me – head-butting me on to further freedom. Like Maria-von-Trapp-to-be, it seems I have no choice. My trance-dance has taken me further than I thought I needed to go. I might have escaped the convent gates, but Life insists I go further.

At the point of scaling a mountainous overhang confidence is in the making, so I do not look down or back at this precarious moment, but continue to climb. A Salamander leads me on through the misty ether rising from the forge of my soul. I need to know the certainty within the make-believe. Climbing over rocks I clamber through the burning fire of the camera lens to get back to the spiritual projectionist of my earthly film – the excellent author of my personal puppet show. It is exhilarating, but difficult, as I continue to dance and ascend.

...When your Heart's on fire, you must realise, smoke gets in your eyes...

Before me the mountain's peak-clouds break and roll threateningly open. Make or break, the engulfing mists bring it all on as the pressure of elements battle in the shaping furnace. Strike upon strike, the mental metal of my Mind's sword is on fire, welling and steaming, regulating the balance between ire and acceptance. An interweaving life of choice and unfolding fate stands before me. I become that which I cannot let go of so I try to remove all the fear and the fault from my experience. I reclaim my Sacred Flame; pulling the Sword-from-the-Stone so that Sorcery White can win.

…What have you done today to make you feel proud?…

The Masters are here up to their old tricks again. In the current mixing of my dream state I do not know whether they belong to the internal or external world. As I attempt to 'let go' and 'let God' the embers of India glow within. I try to put away childish things and surrender to the rising adult energy. Now the mythological, sleeping Serpent stirs holding a flashing ruby in her jaws. The flames flicker, triggering the Dragon's rise up the spine travelling towards the heart, before joining the throat, third eye and crown. Together we Boogie on down the Wonderland and be-bop the divine.

…Karma karma karma karma karma chameleon…if your colours were like my dreams, red, gold and green, red, gold and green…

The diamonds and jewels refract the lighted mirror ball which, bombarded by laser rays, starts to rotate faster. At this speed the Master Rays come into play, spinning many thousands of times faster than a second. The three spiritual E's swallowed earlier in life come back to educate my mind: Explore, Express, Experiment. What wonderful words to lead me on in my meditational dancing, but where in the world have I been spun? Does the answer lie in the ever-gathering mountains of Tibet and Nepal? Is this where we are all divinely begun? Peaks whose views afford the vision of a clear day surround me. If only I can get to stand at the top of their world.

...All the love in the world can't be gone, all the need to be loved can't be wrong...

Geographically lost in the silvery altitudes of mountains that could be the moon, on a glitter ball that could be the globe, on a dance floor that could be Heaven, I instinctively seek out the ancient silk and spice routes and the trading voyage of the buckaroo. My caravan, the H.M.S. Endeavour, is important to me, travelling on highroads to everywhere including the Heart Home where the rising sun rays are like a Breaking Dawn racing across oceans, lands and trees before us. People in search of the Life Force will always find a place to dance and everyone has the right to the essential Earth/Sky energy required for harmonised living in these often troubled times.

...Mr Blue sky, please tell us why, you had to hide away for so long, so long, where did we go wrong...

In search of the Source I breathe through the mists of the dragon's breath. Prana sparkles on the cloud edges of inspiration as the gleaning goes on. As a dancing Dream Catcher I try to capture the in-between states of wake and sleep where we all dream, but I must push on. I pass through the Land of Hypnagogic Air where Gog, Magog and I can dance, weave, and come back to our giant selves. It is a place where things of childhood delight again and where that which is broken can be repaired.

...Red light, spells danger, it's a danger warning...

On the dance floor I spontaneously reclaim and own my body as if celebrating in the streets of Madrid or Seville. Here I am free to trance-dance and go deep into the meditational reverie of me, actively encouraged by Spirit. The quick foot rhythms of a salsa step and the shimmying hip beads of a nearby belly dancer mean I am on fire. A part of me has become higher whereas below, in the sea-forest of fish, folk and flesh, the disco cave heat is sizzling, hot as Hades, Heaven and Hell.

I run through the steam of Guatemalan jungles where Red-Legged Honeycreepers swarm and Hummingbirds hover. Whittington D., a swarthy Brazilian bear admirer, wanders across my path, smiling and dancing like a mad thing. He reminds me of sunlight on water held in the leaves of pre-historically large green plants. He is wonderful and leads me astray from my way. Now on his path I am winding my way through a replenishing rainforest – the Amazonian heart and lungs of the world.

...Upside, inside out...livin' la vida loca...

Elsewhere, the sub-Saharan deserts call to me and the other Wild Men from the Gypsy Mountains. Ferocious, but graceful, they wear flowers in their hair as they bounce and leap around the floor barefooted. Rifles hang from their shoulders. I try to take the aggression and domination of sex and war from out the heart of self and nations. Scents and incense fill our noses from sweet, newly lit firewood and resinous crystals. The English Rose and Spanish Flame entwine. The French and the Americas all join in with sweet thoughts of Liberty and Belle Bonjour.

... "Gypsies, tramps and thieves"...we'd hear it from the people of the town...and lay their money down...

The soft social science of humanity interplays with my imagination. My struggle with Self, hurdles of complexities and a desire for a simpler whole, becomes united in a sublime figure that steadily approaches. My heart opens like a flower. Descending from the mountain the gentle grace of the Buddha is here; Lotus blossom at his naked feet as he runs upon water like a child to the Mother Divine.

...So I'll wait until we're sane, wait until we're blessed and all the same, full of blood, loving life and all it's got to give...

So too, we try to live. Yet I am only one of a hundred, thousand, million dancing selves on the World's dance floor in search of something viewed through the spectrum of hesitating doubt and self-realisation. Are we not all simply auric specks blazing a symphonic trail back home? Momentarily vacillating, I go back to basics in the laboratory of my mind when all feeling tells me of my soul belief of spiritual certainty. Logic drills and speaks in elementary Watson, but is it merely deductive and reductive reasoning trying to overcome intuitive response? Fortuitously, my emotions instinctively kick and rebel as Sense tries to dictate. At this point there is no magic in the restriction of the mind's governing reason.

... 'Cause baby, you're a firework...come on, show 'em what you're worth...make 'em go "oh oh oh!" as you shoot across the sky-y-y...

In the delight of dancing, the answers to the final questions of the former W's 5 are glimpsed and seen, but are instantly lost as a delightful amnesia takes over my struggling mind. God's final dream laugh is like a rolling cloud of heavenly sleeping gas sent from above. Simultaneously, steam rises from my sacral centre, wrapping about me like a warm towel around the loins of a Love God. Mists swirl as they meet and gather.

Through the vapours a Greek playwright, poet and philosopher, an Eastern Yogi, and a mad Man of Welsh-Magic walk forward to greet me. Their wise words and philosophical answers will have to wait for I am too busy dancing. Yet now the everyday obstacles of opposition, restriction and freedom, work and play, battle with confusion and gang up on me – forces and fears from emotions and mind that try to limit. By true nature consciousness, as an evolutionary force, is unlimited, so I work through it all and continue to survey the scene whilst dancing with others.

A chameleon at heart, I change colour and learn through touch and movement, sculptural form, speed and rhythm, their essence. By holding them I can tell who they are, where they have travelled from and where they hope to go. In dancing with them, even for a moment, I know them, and I become further informed of Life's myriad aspects. Yet people will not recognise who I am until I realise myself first, but who am I and what makes a chameleon's core?

Is it the inter-connectedness of souls, defensive camouflage or the Love of All? Is it merely a survival mechanism or is it truly one way of the evolution of love? Perhaps I am happy just fitting in, but why then is this the last dance? Is it the one I have saved for myself to find out the real me or just another self-deceiving illusion? Do I dare take the Divine again as my partner? Do I need some part of me to die to come back to my true self?

...Don't look back, this is your...this is your life...

Dancing, spun so far out from myself, I am but a point in space, a diminishing object between two points – Now and Then, Here and There, Ordinary and Other, Moving yet Still. Adrift, displaced, I am dumbfounded as the celestial planets now seen from above start to move. My natal birth chart is perceived and shown, a basic astrological map of life given for guidance, but we are free to wander where we will. In the end all shall be made well in the return; the rediscovery of known lands through conscious acts of Restitution, joy and a second innocence regained.

Sliding off the seriously circular and the round edges of the Harvest Dream Moon, I find myself back in the Gloop Soup with the rest of the Clangers on the dance floor. However grounded and frustrated, I smile as I look up to see an Ancient Earth Deity stirring the spoon – Goddess Una has hold of the cauldron mix, a melting pot of music and movement. Suddenly, a black soul Mama enters into my body and surprises me. Big-breasted, big-hearted, she is within me and I am left giving birth to gospel, her sermon and her song.

Reparation is made to all states of years past, present and future, as my Night Muse slowly absorbs me back into the Sky Tapestry of Life. Immersed, I fall into the stars' light like a mute, wing-clipped Ancient Angel, smiling, yet death-defying. On the roof of the world, only a Caveman's stick painting remains to depict the honour of the One Dream Maker – Nature and Supernature combined and captured in childlike simplicity and awe.

"Believe gently," the Goddess says soothingly.

In acts of acceptance and reassurance she wipes my brow and I find there is nothing left to do. My final surrender is graceful, even though initially fuelled by chameleon confusion, fight and control. Yet for all my grizzle and for all my grey I fade away like an old, comfy jumper – frayed and over worn with so much friendship and love.

...Fade away and radiate...Oooo baby, watchful lines vibrate soft in brainwave time...

All manner of sleeping debris twists through my newly awakened mind. From within the Moon, the Three Headed Priestess is here to heal, a trinity synthesises in one, followed by a rising Pagan pentagram. Classical and Christian symbols clash in my mind as ancient Cosmological imagery takes hold. The missing evolutionary link of Pan and fauns delight, but the aftermath of the dark angelic wars on Heaven and Earth rumble on enough to make the Lord of Lost Worlds weep.

A man with magic pipes plays and leads me on a merry dance like a free faun encouraging the other satyr spirits and disco sprites to romance, cosmic meltdown and adventure. Mars and Venus peruse the scene; a helmet, shield and lance at rest after the making of Love. Botticelli gladdens the heart as Venus vanquishes Mars. I come to see once again that it is all about Love for without her what are we? From her encompassing bosom a son is formed to suit a male biological form – a cheery, cherry cheek-rouged Cupid with attendant small boyish cherubs.

At this time of the Festival of Winter Trees and Hoary Light I look forward to the promise of Spring and the Maid in the Sea Scallop; she who is fertile and hovers above the depths of the sea. She whispers evolutionary secrets as she lets down her hair. Mermen hang from her tumbling locks eating her oysters. As above, so below. Now I know it is time to go. I move away from the dance floor still shuffling and gliding as though riding the waves of rhythmic water and the translucent light of stars and rays.

An enticing, pearly string of flashing lights hangs from the corridor ceiling and surrounds the door to the beer garden. To me they are the tail of a passing comet, a cluster of good omens within the constellation of the wearying night. I have to follow. They shimmer and lead me to an entrance of a forgotten fairy grotto. Alone now, I go in. Santa Bear is no longer there, but tucked to the back and one side, M'Lady visits and graces us with her presence. As she presides, she pours her moonbeams like purifying water down upon me trying to ease my truth, my hurt, and my anger.

She smiles at me and tries to encourage simple happiness in my present circumstance. A six-sided star heralds all that is good; a rising sign that has journeyed with me through my schoolboy scribbles as well as the doodles and drawings of my adult days. I have followed the star's trail to the milk white presence of She-who-is-Compassion. Big thoughts from the brightest of Moons descend showing me a simple way to grace, understanding, and the several ways of aiding. Any remaining mountain clouds and mists part and evil is simply undone as she shines on down. Somewhere another Good Deed has been done.

Thus absorbed, I pause to look at the Night's bright orb and imbibe her glow. Beyond Christmas fun and fatigue I have been utterly distracted by the merriment of love for the dance. The hours have flown past. Gathering around me in the garden, the other cheery revellers carry on, addicted to Nirvana and the several states of intoxication. Rhythmic ripples rise and fall as we surf our way ever closer toward New Year's Day.

The exhaust of old cycles inhabit our time, but a golden wave of change builds up high for all the Silver Surfers and Cozmic Girlz and Boyz willing to ride the celestial rays. Some Superheroes stand around marvelling at the end of the night, whilst others are lost in the random event of horizon living. Yet the numbers in Light, Time and Space – Astrology, Music and Dance – carry me on to a place where the ancient liberal arts still fascinate. About me, the star cloth of night connecting the dots is now rapidly fading. I am like a smiling cosmonaut waving back at myself through the stars a million planets away. There it is always the Eternal Spring Time of the Cosmic Elf Self.

Thus I become aware that there is a force beyond economics, beyond the exploitation of nations, beyond history and geography, (where history is geography and geography is the living energy of a planet re-emerging and where both must be re-thought in the re-living principle), beyond the trickling fingers on a keyboard and the notes on a stave, beyond the Beyond of the original Big Bang, where lies a common force, both physical and spiritual – which is Time forged into the Love of Motion and Dance.

This many-armed Mistress of the Dance is a compass to the soul, the beat of the Now. She gives and takes. She lifts up, elevates, and breaks down. She disciplines, yet frees, for she is both law and liberation. She calibrates the seconds and the mathematics of poetry, puts planets into motion and teaches the molecules to move. The substantiality of the Cosmos smoothens to her rigour. She celebrates and she grieves. She is sacred and geometric, but is as secular and fluid as the human body allows; every body, for all have the right to own their bodies whether with music or without. She does not lie, but can be manipulated into delightful Rococo and decorative forms if so desired.

She moves, but is as still as the pause between beats as she calculates the social rhythms of dance and sex. She teaches spermatozoa and ova, gametes and zygotes, to swim, flagellating their tails and ovulating their rounds through the fallopian tubes of the Moon and the womb of woman. She connects the quarters, halves, eighths and wholes. She waltzes through the metronome of musical counts to the bugle-wugle boogie-woogie happiness of musical feet. It is a blessing to be whipped up in a moment of divine frenzy with her that is both music and dance combined; a curse to those who must stand by and watch the flapping of my expressive arms and hands in response!

…Ohhh, oh, oh, oh, everybody dance, ohhh oh oh oh, clap your hands, clap your hands…

The Mistress of the Dance both educates and entertains. In her benevolence she teaches tyrants to crawl and children to walk and skip, run, dance and fly. She is the motion of the body, the levers and joints. She is Physics and Spirit alike. She asks the DJs what the workers are listening and dancing to. She sends us the Shakers, the Ecstatics, the lunar tilt of the Epileptics, the Whirl of the Dervishes, and was the untamed teacher to the Berserkers too.

She is in the slide and glide of two-stepping cowpoke everywhere. She is in the Circus, the Carnival Crew, the Geeks and the Freaky Few. She is Saturnalia amok in Morris Men running amuck; they who hold bladders on a stick that bang the folly from our stupid no-brainer bonces. She is clever; but loves the dumbstruck. She is happiness and can be found in the waddle of a bottom of a duck. Every jazz cat knows her stray alley cat strut.

Under the guiding light of a late projected Harvest Moon she takes our hand and offers to dance with us all.

"Shall we dance?" I ask merrily taking hold of a passing moonbeam.

"Dance, dance on 'til dawn," she says. "Then turn and sway; move through another of the Sun's precious days."

So we dance together one final time and pull down once more the Light Divine. Oh yes, we danced all right, all through the night, yet still we could have danced some more. In the dreg ends of the December disco I sense that the finish is near. Some rough diamonds stumble about me, leaping and singing as they gather to leave. It is Time, and I accept that I, Old Man Age, soon must die like the closing of a year. Charred and burnt, I have descended into the gathering ash of memories, ruins and remains. I am so sad to leave it all behind, but none of it can come with me. Especially the thoughts of you – memories linked to an old self that is no longer needed.

…Yeah, it's a new dawn, it's a new day, it's a new life for me, oooooooooh…and I'm feelin' good…

I have crossed the Cosmic Waters and the shored boat, like a chameleon construct, is of no further use and must be left behind. The future jungles call out to the urban monkeys and chimpanzees and I must follow and explore on foot. I cannot be attached to such nostalgic things, but so much fondness and fellowship survive. Yet the mists of time are good, eroding my mountain-conditioned memories and allowing me to renew and start afresh.

My soul set sail many years ago, anchored to my body, and has finally separated and returned to the Eternal Shore. My search for that which is not missing is over, ended in the year end of things, yet restored to Spirit in such a blaze of bright light that furnaces the return of that most strange, healing and colourful of combustible birds – the Phoenix. Burning, falling, but simultaneously rising, ablaze in the forge of consciousness and remembered Awareness, it is ultimately a tale of gunpowder and intrigue which only fireworks know in the showing; the kiss and tell of a Sky Rocket's tail. I check my wristwatch. It is five to five. Is it Friday? It must have been a Chameleon Crackerjack special after all.

The rest of the gang arrives and we explode in the pulling, tumbling about like clowns trying to get our jackets on. The festive frivolities and Christmas detritus still abound. Paper crowns, corny jokes and unwanted surprise presents of who knows what lie all around as we fall out of the stale carryings-on into the refreshing morning. The newness of things wrap around me like a warm, folding jacket in the crisp, cold air after the smoke and smug-fog of the disco environs. I find I am held in your encompassing arms.

Swaggering across car parks we await the renewal of the year and the next day's celebration if we can make it. Perhaps this Chameleon has one more dance left in him after all, if only he can find the energy. Beneath our feet the reflecting stars in Moon-soaked puddles coordinate and guide us on. We go to God messy; inspired living, not negation of self. Strange fruit, strange times, strange tunes cocoon us, warn yet warm us – whilst another inexplicable tale emerges from the deep seed of unpeeling pomegranate me. I struggle with the bursting, but the Yule Log has been lit and we have danced our honour to the fertility of the Stars, the Moon, and to the ancient Stag-Horned God.

How do I share this chaos, this glorious moment of disco debris, damage and delight, with the world? The daybreak birds are tweeting angels harking the early hours and the birth of a new born day even so near to the old year's end. Amidst the Christmas clutter a clear dawn arises alongside a granting of a late present, gift and wish.

I wish you Pilgrim, Friend, as much peace that those in the land of the living can hold; just joy and oh so much love you can grab hold of, and handle, and get wrong. 'Sorry' and 'Thank you' are the only words that the Journeying Soul needs. Do not be afraid to ask for help when those moments of crises arise, for someone will surely come to help you. Even in this Christmas cracker hopefully some crumb of comfort and bliss. What a blowout! What a blast!

Where Life cannot be contained let the vessels shatter, empty and re-shape anew. Let the sharps and shards find their way to the feet of passing Angels. May Grace descend and find you at the centre of a happy life with a star above your stable in elegant slum living. Remember to raise your eyes and look to the skies, just look up, for an ancient star approaches again. The Three Surviving Kings still roam the globe bearing gifts of frankincense, gold epiphany and something special just for you.

Nothing can hold back the Soul's Progress however hard we might fight. Hallelujah right through ya, to you and yours, and so we give it right back to God. For those without God, may your years be filled with Laughter and Love because for you there is only sprawling Life in Abundance – the choosing of personal happiness and the ending of your suffering. If you want a Wonderful Life, be a Wonderful Man or Woman. Do not hold back on your applause. Give and it shall be given. Hold back and you shall remain forever in want, yet know that the Banquet of Love is immense, vaster than fields of flame, mountains and the ups and downs of childhood, however happy or sad. Take from Life's Feast to share and show that you care.

So I raise and sound the new Unicorn's horn that defeats the roaring Lion's claw. Here is to the cornucopia of you and me. Here is to our mutual Prosperity. In my lowly disco descent I find I have climbed Mount Everest and have been blessed again. In ascent I have taken an aeroplane over the Himalayas and that magnificent Moon Mountain named twice: Chomo Lungma and Sagarmatha – sister and brother in one.

Now I must let my Faith and Courage leap once more from the tops of mountains, daring the air in acts of abandonment, stupidity, and adventures of I know not where. Yet now I can ever rest for in my end, Beginning; in my illusions, Truth; in my beingness, Peace; in our shared dream, Awakening.

Health, Peace, and Happiness,

Anam Cara X

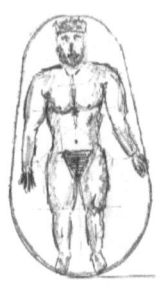

ABOUT THE AUTHOR

Keith Brazil was born in Broadstairs, Kent, England. He trained in Dance Theatre at Laban Trinity Conservatoire, London, and was a founder member of 'Adventures In Motion Pictures' Dance Company. He has worked as a freelance professional dancer, choreographer, teacher, and dance lecturer. Keith has also trained as a Complementary Therapist in Spiritual Healing and Reflexology. He gained a degree in English Studies and is currently engaged in writing a collection of metaphysical and fictional stories, essays, poetry and novels. His first book The Wilderness Diary was published in December 2012. In Consideration of Cats and Popcorn, Parasites, Precious & Pearls were published Autumn 2013. He lives and works in London.